DEBRA ADELAIDE is the author or editor of over twelve books, including the bestselling *Motherlove* series (1996–98) and *Acts of Dog* (2003). Her novels include *The Hotel Albatross* (1995), *Serpent Dust* (1998) and *The Household Guide to Dying* (2008), which was sold around the world. In 2013 she published her first collection of short stories, *Letter to George Clooney*, which was short- and long-listed for three literary awards. Her most recent book is the edited collection *The Simple Act of Reading* (2015). She is an associate professor in creative writing at the University of Technology Sydney.

ALSO BY DEBRA ADELAIDE

NOVELS
The Hotel Albatross
Serpent Dust
The Household Guide to Dying

SHORT STORY COLLECTION
Letter to George Clooney

ANTHOLOGIES
Motherlove
Motherlove 2
Cutting the Cord
Acts of Dog

NON-FICTION
A Bright and Fiery Troop (ed)
Australian Women Writers: a Bibliographic Guide
A Window in the Dark (ed)
Bibliography of Australian Women's Literature
Stories from the Tower (ed)
The Simple Act of Reading (ed)

The Women's Pages

DEBRA
ADELAIDE

PICADOR
Pan Macmillan Australia

First published 2015 in Picador by Pan Macmillan Australia Pty Ltd
1 Market Street, Sydney, New South Wales, Australia, 2000

Cataloguing-in-Publication entry is available
from the National Library of Australia
http://catalogue.nla.gov.au

Typeset in 12.5/17.5 pt Granjon and Doves Type by Post Pre-press Group, Brisbane
Printed by McPherson's Printing Group
Edited by Ali Lavau and Julia Stiles
Internal text design by Sandy Cull, gogoGingko

MIX
Paper from
responsible sources
FSC® C001695

for my daughter

'THAT CAPACITY FOR INTENSE ATTACHMENTS
REMINDED ME OF HER MOTHER:
STILL SHE DID NOT RESEMBLE HER:
FOR SHE COULD BE SOFT AND MILD AS A DOVE . . .'

Emily Brontë, *Wuthering Heights*

❡ WHEN BETTY DENMAN INVITED ELLIS to the barbecue party, they were standing outside the greengrocer's in the early afternoon sun. Its blue canvas awning flapped uselessly against the heat and Ellis was keen to get home, having already been caught up discussing with Gino ways of cooking spinach and why she had never used garlic. And now Betty wanted to chat. She went out every day, making long excursions of activities that other women accomplished in one hit. Ellis imagined her going home after her daily visits to the shops and the post office, to her Wednesday Ladies' Auxiliary meetings and her Friday tennis, always to an empty house until Mack returned from work, at five-forty on the dot. On Saturdays they normally went to the RSL, and on Sundays Betty went to church while Mack played golf.

'Would you mind?' Betty said, adding, 'Your asparagus rolls are almost famous!' as if asking might have been a mild offence.

'Of course not,' Ellis said. She would have offered anyway since she found cooking easy and Betty didn't.

'This Saturday,' Betty repeated. 'Six o'clock. It's for our tenth wedding anniversary.'

She went on to explain that Mack was getting a keg and borrowing the club's punchbowl and cups. And he would be taking the television out the back to set up in his shed, so the men could watch the cricket. Betty didn't seem to notice Ellis checking the baby in the pram, even though he was quiet, and looking up at the hot sky. And she didn't explain why the party seemed to be such a last-minute idea. Ellis briefly wondered at the prospect of Mack organising a party for his and Betty's tenth anniversary. A keg. The club punchbowl. She hadn't heard of a man doing that before.

Finally Ellis checked her wristwatch. 'Betty, I've got to go.'

There was enough time for her to walk home the long way via the corner grocer and finish the shopping and not have to go to the shops again before the weekend. She could get some tins of white asparagus and ask Vince to go out for two fresh loaves first thing Saturday before he left for work, as the baker didn't deliver on the weekend.

Her asparagus rolls *were* almost famous. The secret was using sour cream instead of butter, and forming extra thin slices of bread by first cutting into the loaf from each of the four sides, only as far as the breadknife would go, then severing through the final middle portion. You could get wafer-thin slices that way. Along with the finely ground black pepper, and the sour cream spread that Ellis made herself, this technique made all the difference, though none of the other women could ever work out why. Hardly anyone thought to use black pepper, and as far as Ellis could tell no one but she used sour cream much. It was the sort of thing women tended to buy when they made beef stroganoff, but she generally kept a carton in the fridge and used it in all sorts of dishes.

By the time she got home the air in the flat, which trapped the afternoon sun, had become thick with heat. She took the baby out of his pram and into his room. Charlie was damp but still drowsy so she put him straight into his cot without changing his nappy, switching on the corner fan and covering him with a sheet.

In the kitchen she opened the window over the sink and pulled the blind halfway down, then took out the potatoes, half a savoy cabbage and beans from the string bag she had hung over the handles of the pram. She put the meat and sour cream in the fridge and smoothed out the sheets of newspaper the greengrocer had wrapped the cabbage in and stored them in the box beneath the sink to use later for lining the bin. The cabbage had received a faint imprint of news ink on its cut side. Gino always used the *Daily Telegraph*, but she wished he would not wrap cut vegetables in the front page, as its larger type was so much more inky. She could see a trace in reverse of the headlines about the referendum on the casino in Tasmania.

She looked at the cabbage for a while, considering whether to wash it or shave the spoiled side off, but left it on the draining board instead. Vince loved savoy cabbage lightly boiled and smothered in butter, though she resisted cooking it at all, if possible: ever since boarding school the smell had repelled her. Gino had offered her a vegetable he called an eggplant, which he said his father grew in their backyard. He had told her it tasted like oily heaven and she was intrigued, cupping the glossy purple globe in her hand, especially when he said his family cooked it in a vegetable casserole dish called caponata. She repeated it, cap-on-a-ta, a lovely new word which sounded like a musical term. And a vegetable casserole, something even newer. But she knew Vince would not like it.

Finally, she placed the tins of asparagus in the cupboard, closed the door, and rested her forehead against it, staring at the laminex bench below for a long time. A ten-year anniversary. The laminex, pale green, was worn in places but not likely to be replaced as she and Vince were only renting. She rubbed at some whorls of scratches inflicted by a previous tenant. She could not imagine ten years of marriage. When she had accepted Vince she had known it was not for love but had believed it was the right thing for her to do. However, ever since the baby had arrived the great injustice of what she had done rose like a tide of bile up her throat. Some days it was as if she had literally to swallow down on the bitterness of how fraudulent she felt. Miserable, too, as she knew Vince deserved better. Ten years. She could not foresee another eight years like this.

Had there not been a sudden wail from the baby's room she might have cried herself. She listened to Charlie's sobs for a minute before breathing in deeply and turning around. Her son was only six months old and she had no right to present him with the cold truth stamped all over her face. In his room, smiling, she reached out for him, kissing his teary face quiet. She tucked him close into her neck, cradling his now sodden bottom in her other hand.

'It's going to be tough, little one,' she whispered as she laid him down and prepared to undress him for his bath.

2

―――――

❡ IT WAS READING THAT HAD BROUGHT
Dove to this. Reading that novel when she was a teenager, or
whenever it was she had first read it, then again as a young
woman, when she had underlined great slabs of the text in
ink, for some reason she could not now remember, and then
yet again to her mother as she lay in hospital dying – reading it
had infected her imagination. It was like a malaria of the brain,
lying dormant then leaping up at unexpected times to attack
with the fever of unresolved narrative. And it would not depart
until she had grappled with the confusion of gaps and shadowy
images and half-truths – ones that were far more dominant and
demanding than the scenes and the characters that she also saw
with perfect, often frightening, clarity.

The novel had unfolded again and again to be something

different every time, and she was sick of it because it meant there would never be a final reading of this book for her. Like that mosquito-borne tropical fever, it would never let her go. She had half a lifetime ahead of her, she was not yet forty, and this novel was going to torture her for the rest of her life. She would be close to death and it would still have its hooks into her. Doubtless even after death when she was good and buried with the soft wind breathing through the grass above her, not for her would there be peace. She would never be one of the sleepers in the quiet earth.

Nevertheless Dove bought the copy of *Wuthering Heights* that afternoon. It was impossible not to even though she already had several copies at home. She had gone into town to buy a new coffee machine and ended up in Dymocks where the stand of Penguin Classics lured – no, taunted – her. And on the bus going home she re-read the first three chapters. By the time she got off and walked down the street and into her house, she felt as exhausted and benumbed as Lockwood, feeble as a kitten and wishing she had her own housekeeper to bring in supper and sit down with her while she ate it, and either animate or lull her to sleep with her talk.

Her mother had been a violin teacher, and when she was lying peaceful and close to death in hospital Dove had suggested some music, thinking she could bring in her iPod and feed it straight into her ears. But Jane had requested, murmuring, that she bring in *Wuthering Heights* and read it to her instead. And she wanted the old copy from her flat. When Dove found

it she saw that it was stamped on the inside cover with the name
of the girls' school past Bathurst where her mother had taught
music nearly forty years ago, before she was born. Perhaps she had
taught English as well, since the copy contained tiny slips with
notes and pencilled annotations in the margins – her mother's
discreet hand was nothing like her own bold underlinings and
exclamation marks. *A novel without a reader?* went one neat
comment on the half-title page. Another noted, *Imptc of narrative
perspective. Self-conscious literary artefact.* On the facsimile
reproduction of the 1847 title page, her mother had written next
to the pseudonym Ellis Bell, *Distancing: Brontë/Bell/Lockwood/
Nelly/etc.* As she leafed through it, catching the sweet dusty scent
of its tea-coloured pages, a note fell out. *Chapt 16: C dies halfway
through novel*, it stated. *Absent mother theme reinforced.*

Dove had almost sniffed at that, refusing to consider the
obvious. Her mother wanted this book read to her and so she
would read it to her. And what had happened was not just that
her mother had died with the sound of Emily Brontë's words
quietly spoken into her ear, but that Dove had found a story,
followed it, and was now firmly trapped within it.

Or so it felt. She was a graphic designer and thought in
images, not words. She read the novel and saw scenes vividly.
And even as she slept she saw people and events unfolding, and
during the weeks in which she read the book to her mother a
character called Ellis and her story emerged with such clarity it
became a compulsion for her to write. Before they had finished
reading the book she had made notes and drafted out scenes in

a purple notebook her mother had given her some time before she had become ill. Writing late at nights after she returned from her hospital visits, or in the early hours of the day, she had not really stopped to question where the story was going or even why she – who had never before harboured a desire to write – was now gripped by a feverish, urgent need to find out what this story was about and where it would end.

As her mother's life had slowly ebbed away after her final debilitating stroke, Dove had been creating another narrative which commenced by describing an event in the life of Ellis, a young married woman travelling on a bus with her baby Charlie, to visit her father in Ashfield. She saw this powerfully, vividly, much of it unfolding before her like a film. She saw clearly the suburb of Ashfield and knew it was the late 1960s, and caught a strong sensual impression of the place: the smells from the gardens, from the kitchens, on that particular day. All this was so strong that Dove wondered if she had ever lived in a house similar to Ellis's father's house, back before she could remember. It was a Federation place with a front garden featuring an old wire gate and a fence covered in plumbago. A tessellated path led up to the front verandah. There were houses and gardens like this in Ashfield still, she knew, because she'd been there recently, researching for the story.

In one way the story began simply: Ellis was making a regular weekly visit to her father who lived alone, and she was taking the bus because she did not drive, not uncommon for women back then. Nothing much happened. Some elderly women on the bus disapproved of the fact that the baby was underdressed, despite the heat of the day, and was not wearing his hat. The most momentous thing was when Ellis placed Charlie down on the path at her father's house and he took his first steps.

It was while Dove was writing this part of the story that her mother began to die. She was quickly writing this section down on her laptop, seated by her mother's bed, when she heard the unmistakable noises heralding imminent death, the labour of breath. At the same time she realised two things: it was the reading aloud of the novel that had helped her understand it better, and that this had somehow inspired the story she was writing. And she understood nothing more than that, but in any case why would she? She had more important things to contend with: her mother, who had been so quiet for weeks, was now breathing louder and louder, desperate to grasp hold of some final moments of life, as the dying often do.

*

THAT WAS NEARLY A YEAR AGO, when her mother died. Dove had taken so much leave from her job, then given it up altogether, grieving and settling Jane's affairs, and then continuing to write the story because it seemed the only thing to do. Now there were patterns in it and structural complexities that had made her despair that it would all ever click properly into place. And there were uncanny personal connections. For instance, until lately she had never thought about the pattern that saw Ellis without a mother while she herself became an orphan. Or the fact that in the weeks before her mother died she was negotiating to transfer her to a nursing home called The Grange (which never happened: Jane remained in the palliative care ward of her local hospital). Thrushcross Grange was clearly in her mind, but then Dove had not invented the nursing home in Strathfield, surely?

Now the story was all drafted it was still in need of pulling apart and serious rethinking. Dove had Charlie walking early on, but that would mean he was about one, whereas in the parts she had written next, a barbecue scene, he was only about six months old. This was the problem, she guessed, of seeing things clearly but in complete scenes, like sequences cut out of a film. Were she a real writer maybe she would know how to plan it, to write it chronologically, but already she could see it was far too late for that.

Parts of it had come in dreams. Of course she was not so naive or inexperienced an author to think that a dream could be translated directly onto the page and somehow make fictional sense, and she puzzled for a while over the meaning of these dreams, wondering if they even had any relevance to the story in her head. Eventually she simply wrote the dreams as she recalled them and put them aside to think on. When she did incorporate them, she was quite pleased with how they seemed to fit naturally into the narrative. One of the dreams described how in her sleep she was reaching out to rescue Ellis from being dumped in a roadside ditch, in the early hours of a morning. Dove was heaving and dragging her out of the earth in a remote and harsh landscape somewhere, a place of dark, low sky, scrubby grass and few trees. She revived her, brushed the cold earth off her, and restored her to life. Images of burial and suffocation in the earth were understandable, given the content of *Wuthering Heights.*

She soon stopped puzzling over why this novel led her to a story about a young woman with a baby. All she knew was that Ellis – the inspiration for her name obvious – despite being like the fourth or fifth figure in a set of babushka dolls, was as real to her, a new author, as if she had bumped into her alighting that bus in a street in Ashfield on a warm summer morning in 1968. But what Ellis did next surprised even her.

3

⸿ DRIVING OUT OF THEIR STREET ON
Saturday evening on their way to the barbecue, Ellis felt more
sad than anything. She periodically turned around to inspect
the back seat where the platter of asparagus rolls rested next
to Charlie in his portable bassinet. The asparagus rolls were
garnished in parsley and covered in a damp tea towel. You could
cover food with greaseproof paper if you wanted, but for dishes
like this Ellis always used a damp cloth. It meant, in summer
especially, the food would never dry out.

As the car turned a corner, she felt a small stab of something
that should have been guilt but she knew was not. She would
have preferred walking to Betty and Mack's, on her own,
briskly, to clear her head if that were possible, or at least to feel
the freedom of her body moving at pace. But Vince had worked

until after five and they would have been late. And one of them would have had to carry the platter of asparagus rolls. Besides, you couldn't arrive anywhere separately, least of all your friends' anniversary party. Nor would she have been able to wear her new slingbacks. She looked down at them with satisfaction; they were camel coloured, patent leather, smart but not too high in the heel. Vince opened his window a little wider. One arm, bare and tanned, encircled the steering wheel while he leaned the other on the window. A stiff breeze tumbled through the car. She could smell his Aqua Velva aftershave, a Christmas present, and the dust from the street, the tarry road, and a whiff of something organic – the garbage bins from the strip of local shops they were now passing. There was a milk bar, the newsagency, a dry cleaner's and a garden shop, which was barely a business, more the converted front yard of someone's house, and which she'd never been into. Vince went to the newsagency for his Sunday paper and the cigarettes, but Ellis did her shopping farther down towards the main road. The Annandale shops had everything she needed, and only occasionally she went all the way to Parramatta Road and caught the bus to town. Once a week she took the bus in the opposite direction to visit her father in Ashfield.

It was a beautiful evening, cicadas shrieking in the plane trees nearby. Dusk was beginning to settle and the pink-flushed sky promised more of the same warmth the next day. The uneasy feeling Ellis felt developed so quickly into such acute realisation that, when it struck her, she couldn't believe Vince hadn't noticed. She felt ill with it, in the middle of her stomach.

'You okay?'

He had noticed, then.

'Yes,' she said, taking her hand off her stomach and twisting around to look at the back seat again. 'Charlie's good,' she added, just for something to say.

If I think about it any more he'll know, she thought. If I confront it tonight of all times, the fact that I cannot live with him any more, he will ask me what is wrong. She pushed the thought as far off as she could. He and Mack were old mates, having done their mechanical training together, despite Mack being a good ten years older. Mack and Betty were decent people. Their party would also be full of decent people, uncomprehending types who would never understand someone like her, who every day of her life now had to swallow down hard and in silence the bitterness of her choice.

She breathed in deeply but quietly and looked out the window. Vince reached over to push the cigarette lighter in, then fumbled in his top pocket.

'Open it for me, will you, love?'

It was new packet, bought earlier for the evening out. Apart from his breakfast cigarette, Vince rarely smoked during the day and never while he was at work, unlike the other mechanics. She tore the strip off the cellophane, prised out the silver paper and extended one of the cigarettes, then handed him the packet. Her face remained unflushed, her hand refused to shake. But all the while her stomach beat with a low rhythm, flooding her body with a sensation that was curiously both empty and full.

She wondered what happened to women like her, because there was no excuse, none whatsoever. Vince was dependable and thoughtful. He was the sort of man women wanted for a husband. Ellis should have felt more shame and guilt than she did – and then she felt guilty and shameful for not doing so. But already she was thinking of how she would have to get a place. Probably she would just move back in with her father for a while, if he would have her. She would have to return to office or retail work. It had been a few years now, but the chemist shop might even take her back.

*

THE PARTY WAS PREDICTABLE. As always Betty had tried hard with the food, but if only she didn't feel the urge to experiment, Ellis thought. Mack insisted on barbecuing, as was his male right, but hadn't an idea of how to cook even a sausage. The three or four times Ellis had been a guest at the Denmans', the meat had been ritualistically burnt. Mack had the primal conviction of his gender that chops and steaks needed cooking into submission. And something to do with the cricket had meant his mind wasn't on the job anyway. The television set was fuzzy, and a man she didn't know was up a ladder at the corner of the shed fiddling with a makeshift aerial. Ellis inspected the T-bone steaks incinerating beside a mound of black sausages, and then continued helping Betty hand around dishes. Even though it was a barbecue, Betty had produced canapés using the *Women's Weekly Cookbook* that Mack had bought her for Christmas. Despite that, the cheese straws tasted doughy. And Ellis decided there and then she would be happy never to see an angel on horseback again. Several people asked for her to return with her platter of asparagus rolls, but they had vanished quickly. The mushroom vol-au-vents, chewy and wobbly at the same time, sat ignored on the table outside until Ellis took them over to some of the other women.

'Betty cooked them,' she said with meaning. Three of the church friends – Ellis didn't remember their names – obediently took one each. Down the back, the men ate potato chips and drank beer from the keg beside the shed. The television glowed like an underwater light in the dark of the shed.

Party lights were strung across the porch and around the Hills Hoist, illuminating the faces of those sitting around in eerie primary colours. Three women were crammed into the canopied garden seat that was pressed too hard against the back wall for swinging, their heads bathed in alien green. Next to them two of Betty's older friends from tennis were seated in deckchairs, nursing lemonades with almost pointed temperance. Just by glancing at their faces Ellis knew that these two had been discussing Betty's last miscarriage. The others were talking about the prime minister's personal secretary, all these months after her appointment. Ellis admired Ainsley Gotto: she was so young, not much older than Ellis herself.

'Apparently she smokes cigars!' one woman said.

'Yes,' Ellis said. 'How amazing is that?' Then, judging the mood, held out her hands for the empty wooden nut bowls. 'Can I take them?' she said before anyone else could speak. Three sets of eyes followed her as she went inside with the bowls to look for the potato chips.

At the door she realised the back of the house had become dark in the past hour, as no one had come in. Along the hall there was a sliver of light from under the door of the front room, where the children were playing board games and one of the older girls was minding Charlie. She heard a noise in the kitchen and saw Betty sitting at the kitchen table, pressing a serviette to her eyes. Ellis stepped over behind her and held her lightly across the shoulders for a few moments. Then she switched on the kitchen light and quickly disposed of the uneaten potato salad – with condensed milk mayonnaise, how could Betty have done that? – and the half-eaten cheese straws, and sat beside her, listening to the children in the front room chattering over a game of Scrabble. Betty stared at the serviette before pressing it to her face again. Crescents of black mascara had come away against the red and white checked cloth.

'I'm sorry,' Ellis said, rubbing Betty's shoulder again, but knowing there was really nothing she could say. No kind words existed to erase the pain.

'Never mind.' Betty screwed up the serviette then stood and went over to the sink where she poured a glass of water which she drank in one go. She turned around and heaved in a lungful of air, an Olympic champion facing down the final lap.

'Don't say anything to Mack, will you?' She went to the bathroom and shut the door.

Later, Ellis was standing at the kitchen sink, hands in soapy water, getting a start on the dishes. Although the cricket was over, Vince was still parked in front of the television. She supposed he would insist he was right to drive home. Betty had returned to the backyard, foraging for dirty plates and beer glasses, but Ellis knew she would get distracted talking and forget the greasy plates in her hand. Her laugh was a silvery trilling thing that shot up the garden like a small bright bird, a canary or finch, something that had escaped from confinement but was nervously looking to hide again.

There was movement behind Ellis, a creak of floorboard under lino. A heavy cut-glass bowl dripped suds down her hands as she held it up out of the water. Before she realised it, before she registered the smell of tobacco – Champion Ruby, quite fragrant really – she felt the pressure around her waist. Betty still used yellow soap in a wire holder, which meant the dishes were very slippery. And they would streak without a good rinsing. Ellis felt a hardness pressed into her back, at the same time as her hair was lifted to one side and lips, beery wet, sucked at her neck. She placed the bowl, very carefully, in the dish rack, and turned around. She had brushed past him collecting scraps from the trestle table.

'Les. Shove off. You've had too much to drink.' She leaned back against the sink, daring him to touch her again.

He held out his arms, smiling. Ellis had caught his eye once or twice before, and could not believe that a husband of one of Betty's church friends would behave like this.

'Come on. You know you want me.' He stepped back, arms still out, as if to say, Look at me, how can you resist?

She peeled off the pink rubber gloves – she would not leave wet handprints on him – and dropped them on the draining board.

'Just go,' she said.

He came closer again, gripped her by the shoulders. His breath was urgent and demanding with alcohol, his voice pleading.

'But I love you. You're gorgeous.'

She would not call out or even remonstrate with him, though she felt like it. The crushed serviette Betty had used on her eyes was still on the kitchen table where she had sat in the dark. Now Ellis heard her laughter fluttering around again from out in the garden, followed by a series of tinny clinks. Someone throwing beer bottles into the garbage bin.

He was an abject sight. She pushed him away. Both hands on his chest, firmly. No wet handprints. And took them back again quickly before he could grab them and place them further down.

'No. You just don't love your wife.'

His wife – was she out there in the dark garden? Ellis couldn't recall, but she sometimes worked night shifts at the convalescent home. Ellis almost changed her mind but even as she opened her mouth to call Vince, Mack, anyone, she saw Betty's crumpled face. And here was Les's cheery innocence. His likeability. The fact that they were alone in the kitchen. She heard the clink of glass again. The keg had run out an hour before. She glared at Les, who stopped smiling. His mouth set in a line, he patted his top pocket and pulled out his tobacco and papers and started rolling with quick firm fingers. As he looked down she noticed a blooming bald patch. That he was quite short, really. She sighed. How could she almost feel sorry for him?

'Don't know what's up your arse, love.' He stuffed the cigarette into his mouth, struck a match and lit it, his eyes slits as he drew back on the smoke. 'Suppose you've just always been a tight bitch.'

Ellis turned around, yanked the plug out of the sink and squeezed the Wettex until it shrank dry, and when she turned again he was gone. She wiped her hands meticulously on a clean tea towel, then went out to the back patio and down the garden to the shed.

'We need to go home now,' she said to Vince. 'I'll go and organise Charlie.'

4

⟪ DOVE HAD NEVER HAD MUCH TIME FOR cooking and she wondered how her main character was so plausibly domestic. Here was Ellis having made a huge platter of asparagus rolls and when Dove wrote the details of her secret recipe it was as if she had been making them herself all her life. She had never even eaten an asparagus roll, she thought, and had certainly never made them. She felt like she was in the back seat as Vince drove Ellis out of their street to the Denmans' barbecue, that she might have been spotted by Ellis as she was turning around to check on Charlie. His portable bassinet was strapped to the bench seat with an old belt of Vince's that Ellis had adapted, not trusting the bassinet alone would hold Charlie safe, even though everyone did it.

Dove had written enough of this story by now to understand

there was a pattern, not in the story so much – she despaired there would ever be a pattern – but in the way she approached it. Or it her. She could see scenes quite clearly, but then after writing them down she would see them all over again from different angles. And these angles would offer new images. In this way she now saw what was only fuzzy the first time round, which was the baby lying peacefully as Vince drove. Charlie was not far off sitting up on his own, and had he not already been sleepy Ellis would have needed to hold him in her lap. As it was he settled down the minute the car set off, the rhythm as always a comfort. There was still a lot of heat in the air so Ellis had soaked a clean tea towel, wrung it out and placed it over the asparagus rolls to prevent them from drying out.

It had been very hot earlier in the week, too, when Ellis had bumped into Betty Denman. She had been extra anxious that day to get home and put Charlie down for his nap in his room with the fan. By the time she had got home he had almost been asleep and she had lifted him from his pram into his cot without bothering to change his nappy, before putting away the shopping. This was tricky because like a lot of mothers Ellis had looped the string shopping bag over the handles of the pram (the parcel of meat she'd tucked behind Charlie's head, to keep out of the sun), and removing the baby first threatened to topple the pram backwards. Dove kept an eye on it, parked in the hallway, while Ellis turned on the fan and lowered the blind in the nursery, half expecting that Ellis would emerge to a mess of broken eggs and a split sour cream carton, the potatoes rolling down the hall like misshapen bowling balls.

Dove began revising the barbecue chapter, stopping for typos and fiddling with punctuation, until she realised she had some serious questions to consider. For instance, was the cricket transmitted on television in early 1968? She thought perhaps not and, having captured the other details of Ellis's world, was obliged to follow this through. She would have to consult the newspapers, or the TV guides. That would mean a trip to the library. But the more she thought about it she doubted the cricket would be on in the evening anyway. Where would they be playing cricket after dark?

She pulled out the purple notebook and began a list of things like that needing verification. The Aqua Velva was an odd touch: she had no idea where that had come from, but she knew it was a popular men's aftershave at that time, like Old Spice, and like Brut was in the 1970s when she was a child. Where that detail had come from, she had some idea: she could even remember the catchy TV jingle, *Where, where, where would you be without Brut 33?*, and her singing it in the bath when she was just a little girl, three or four. The Aqua Velva, she decided, was a Christmas present to Vince from Charlie, his very first. Ellis would have written on the card in a pretend child's hand.

As she re-read the scene she had drafted she wondered about Ellis and Les. How realistic was it? And yet there again was the undeniable sensation of having peered into a character and seen her entire life, her story, her personality, as complete as it would ever be. And while Dove knew she alone had hauled this person Ellis out from the black soil of her imagination, she also knew she was incapable of altering a thing about her. It was as if she were merely responsible for getting her breathing again, brushing off the dirt, and sending her on her way.

In truth she had felt almost nervous when she had written that Ellis was contemplating ending her marriage. Ellis was dependable. She was responsible, a homemaker since she was sixteen, and had never let anyone down in that respect, her husband or her father before that. As a daughter she was both loving and dutiful: after she had recovered from the birth and become organised enough to travel on the bus with a small baby, she had been visiting her father every week. Vince had married her when she was working and studying part time and had not questioned her giving up either. Nothing in this story hinted at Ellis's profound misery.

*

DOVE SHUT THE NOTEBOOK and went to make a cup of coffee. As she reached into the fridge she heard the bleat of her mobile phone from the front room where she had left it the night before. It needed charging, but she ignored it. No one wanted her urgently now, or if they did they could email her or use the home phone. Work no longer contacted her: she had taken so many days off, then gone to half weeks, then taken leave altogether, but her office friends (if that's what they were) seemed relieved not to have to deal with her unconventional behaviour: instead of wilting in tears she had become steely and detached in pursuit of this story. Other people, she was advised, took cruises or cleared out houses or found new hobbies to cope with grief. She was just retreating into words.

But she didn't care what they thought, she was functioning. Before the story claimed her this morning she had been intending to do the laundry and take the cat to the vet. Since her mother had died she had no idea if he needed vaccination or worming. She had never owned a cat. But then the day was kind, and the cat seemed perfectly healthy. He was sunning himself on the back porch, and Dove thought she would look over her story again, and now here it was past midday. She made the coffee and took it out to drink on the porch. The cat – she still forgot to think of him by his name – nudged her arm. His name was Viv, short for Vivaldi, a mouthful for a mere cat, she always thought. But then even her mother had called him Viv.

He made noises like a baby, and in some ways was as demanding. Not that Dove had any idea of looking after a baby either. And as for the noises, she had only imagined what Charlie sounded like, having of course never heard him. But she knew he was a manageable child, so much so that Ellis and Vince had settled into an easy routine. After dinner she always got Charlie off to bed and tidied his things while Vince did the dishes, but even before the baby came along he helped around the house.

Hence the terrible conflicting emotions in Ellis as she dealt with the realisation, that evening, that she could no longer live with a man she did not love.

Dove saw her again in Betty's kitchen: almost on cue there was a wail from the front bedroom, where one of the older girls had offered to settle Charlie to sleep with a bottle. Ellis had realised that with her baby so healthy, so palpably here, she was perhaps the worst enemy to poor Betty Denman. Later that evening when she went to fetch him, just after telling Vince they had to leave, he was asleep in the arms of Betty's niece. Ellis decided then she would have to enlist her father to help with Charlie when she went back to work.

Dove rubbed Viv's head, hot from the sun. The encounter with Ellis and Les struck her as being entirely plausible, the more she considered it, but only if she worked harder at it. Already the story had become too complex, and leaped around in time. She needed to go further back, and think more carefully about the start. If there was one.

5

WHEN SHE RETURNED FROM BOARDING school for the last time, soon after turning sixteen, Ellis found her father had aged. He was still working at the bank and active in his bowls club, but she thought now how old he was, his hair very grey and thin. All the girls at school had fathers who were much younger than hers.

Since she was so capable there was no need to employ their housekeeper any longer but someone needed to run the place for him, a man who didn't cook or shop. For the four years Ellis had been at boarding school, Mrs Wood had come around with prepared meals and done the weekly cleaning and laundering for Edgar. Before that she had come every day in the morning and prepared Ellis's breakfast and taken her to school, then met her again at the school gate in the afternoon and brought her home to prepare dinner until her father returned from work.

Now Ellis took charge of the small household. By that stage she found the kitchen as old-fashioned as Mrs Wood had – her school's domestic science rooms had featured double stainless steel sinks and electric St George stoves. Their kitchen did not boast a single electric appliance and indeed Mrs Wood had complained when she'd had to plug the iron into the one power point above the bench, which she considered unsafe. She had always brought along her own electric beaters, a Sunbeam handheld, to beat egg whites into snowy peaks for a lemon meringue pie, which was Edgar's favourite dessert, or if Ellis were lucky, a pavlova. Sometimes as a treat she'd allow Ellis to hold the beaters for the final few minutes while she eyed the power point with suspicion. Mrs Wood now worked for Strathfield Council as a demonstrator, showing housewives the marvels of things like electric frypans that could cook an entire family roast using a fraction of the power of a normal oven.

Three nights a week, Ellis attended the technical college, learning typing and shorthand in the commercial department. Her father had suggested this plan, rather than taking the day classes, as that way she could get an office position and also learn on the job. He had not particularly cared that she become qualified for anything, or gain employment, since to him the house represented enough of an occupation. But one of the wonderful things about her father was that he did not pressure her nor force his opinions on her. Perhaps he understood something of the changing world, sniffed it in the air, and realised that now, a whole generation after the war, after everything had been turned upside down and inside out, after women had driven trams and worked night shifts making ammunition parts and represented constituents in parliament and run their own electrical engineering companies, there could never be a turning back.

At school she had been lucky enough to encounter a couple of teachers who were intelligent and well qualified, who suggested by example rather than outright instruction that there was something more to life than running a house. The irony for Ellis, something she began to feel consciously when she returned from boarding school to commence her adult life, was that she was so very competent at this. And, despite her enthusiasm, untalented when it came to music, or dance, or any of the finer creative pursuits, except for arts and crafts. It would be too easy, she realised, to slip into the role of minding house for her father, then later in life, in his older years or after his death (not that she particularly wanted to think about that), to find she was a spinster with nothing more than a weekly bridge game or tennis to look forward to. Sardines on toast for Saturday dinners – because otherwise why would a person on their own be bothered? – knitting cardigans for charities, and the Tuesday matinée movie.

The other girls at school planned to become teachers themselves, or to do nursing. A small number went on to something called finishing school, in the city, which Ellis understood to be a place where girls practised walking with books on their heads, or learned the correct order of cutlery for banquets. She had no desire for anything in particular, but only knew she was not suited for teaching, had no interest in emptying bedpans and anyway was squeamish when it came to syringes and blood. And certainly she could not see the need for learning how to cross her legs elegantly, or that sprinkling sliced tomato with sugar made for a better sandwich. These were the sorts of things that, in her view, should come pretty naturally to any reasonably intelligent young woman.

Going through the list of courses on offer at the technical college, she rejected Hairdressing and Floristry, Cookery and Craftwork on similar grounds: she did these things all the time and had done since she was a girl.

She had placed the college's brochure down on the kitchen table one night, next to her father, waiting while she served the dinner. Fried chops and cauliflower in cheese sauce, one of his favourites.

'I don't need to learn more cookery,' she said. 'I already know how to fold beaten egg whites for a soufflé.' She pointed to the illustration and laughed.

'What about this? You like flowers.' He pointed to Floristry.

'An uneven number of rose stems makes for a pleasing display,' she read out. 'I don't think so, Dad.'

He adjusted his glasses and read up and down the list before putting the brochure down and tapping hard at the last course listed.

'Typing,' he said, 'and general secretarial skills. That would be handy.'

Later, when Ellis thought about it, she realised he was right. Besides, it would be something new.

At times like this she yearned to ask her father what her mother had done, who she had been, but all her life she had known that was a forbidden topic. Had her mother been artistic, fashionable, practical? Was she a nurse or a librarian or just a young woman like so many young women, someone who marked time working in a shop or minding children until their real career came along and they married?

In her bedroom that night she had stared into the dressing table mirror, perhaps the same mirror of the same dressing table her mother had used. When she was younger Ellis would gaze fiercely into this mirror, into her own dark blue eyes, at her dark brown hair, trying to will her mother's image into being, wondering if there was any similarity at all. Tonight she felt almost angry at the thought. Her mother had gone away and left her when she was just a baby. She would be nothing like her mother, nothing at all. She hoped her mother, whoever she was, wherever she now lived, had never made a perfect soufflé or known how to knit in bobble stitch, as Ellis did thanks to Mrs Wood.

She would be more than domestically accomplished. After finishing her secretarial certificate she planned to take bookkeeping and accountancy, though so far she had peeked into the rooms of those classes on her way to Miss Allman's

Tuesday night typing class and seen only men in the lecture rooms of the Mary Ann Street premises. But after the revision exercises and the practice typing she did on a dummy keyboard at home, her hands covered in a black cloth and her eye on the clock, Ellis found that her days stretched out. If her father had not been there to make tea for, or to check that his bowling gear was all clean and pressed, his sandwiches packed and thermos filled, then she might have howled inside that large cool house, howled for the suffocation, the hollowness, of her life at sixteen.

6

⟨ WHEN SHE WAS AT UNIVERSITY, DOVE had settled in with a small group of friends who were mainly older than she. Perhaps it was her single-child status, or her mother's relaxed style of parenting which meant she had rarely been constrained by rules in the ways other children she knew seemed to be, but she had always felt older than she was, and uncomfortable around people her own age. Most of her classmates struck her as immature and boring. Their madcap escapades – illicit parties in the colleges, nude midnight runs around the ovals, or quests to find the most bogan clubs in the outer suburbs – seemed to dominate their imagination. One acquaintance found hilarity in seeking out the most unreconstructed cafés in town, dragging everyone off to places with laminex and studded vinyl booths to eat meals like minute steak with tinned mushrooms in sauce, served with white bread and margarine. Look, he would say, curried sausages! A pie and tinned peas! They were all meant to exclaim over the meals, even the menus themselves, typed crookedly and in sticky plastic folders. After the second adventure she could not see the point, while the sight of the proprietors of these places, always a Greek or Italian husband-and-wife team, dressed in grease-spattered white overalls, hovering uncertainly between humiliation and delight at the sudden patronage, disturbed her.

She knew her friends thought her boring too. Nerdy and straight. But she actually liked attending classes, enjoyed her studies. To her university was not a place to be endured while the rest of life went on in bars or at the beach or down the snow in winter, it was her life. Art and design were exciting. Sometimes she even found it thrilling. The mature age students were the only ones who seemed to share this. They were a loose knot of friends, coming together after lectures in a corner of the university's central coffee lounge to share notes or flip through magazines. Sometimes they wandered up to Newtown to see a movie at the Dendy, or they walked down to get cheap meals in Chinatown. But they didn't visit each other's homes and never went away together. There were a couple of tighter strands in this knot of acquaintances. One of these was Martin, a tall gaunt man who never smiled, who was studying architecture, but distractedly as if something else were always on his mind. Later Dove learned he had switched degrees, having nearly completed civil engineering. Another was a fey woman who dressed in

long velvety skirts and always wore hats, even in lectures. Martin
had an alarming yet admirable habit of appearing at lectures
to announce some event, student or political, the sort of thing
that did not interest Dove, making the lecturer wait on the side
of the podium while he finished his speech. He would then
lope away to some other more important activity and never, as
far as Dove recalled, attended his lectures. Angela, the velvety
woman, would sit in the front row and interrupt with questions.
Dove wondered if these people's ages conferred a status on them
in the eyes of their teachers. She would never have dared skip
classes or ask questions. Martin and Angela trailed numerous
friends behind them, what with their political activities, and
in Angela's case, her tarot card readings and reputation for
benign witchcraft. Dove was inclined to be suspicious of them
both, but her desire for friends, or perhaps her suppressed fear
of being friendless, kept her in check. And they were pleasant
enough to her. Or they were not unpleasant.

She became accustomed to meeting them in the student
coffee lounge, where they were sometimes sitting with a much
younger man. For the first few times Dove and he never spoke.
These were not the sorts of gatherings where people were
necessarily introduced to each other. One day after lunch the
booth was unusually full, and Martin and Angela arrived just
as some others were leaving. They stood around sipping their
coffees, Angela flicking her long black hair over her shoulder,
waiting to slide into a seat. Martin was consulting some papers.
He always had papers and manila folders, held loose so that they

often slipped to the floor. He gave the impression that his entire life, like his arms, was profoundly cluttered, as if his intellect and imagination were so far reaching, so broad and diverse, that they could not be contained by the organisational tools of lesser students, such as Dove, with her colour-coded ring folders and Post-it notes. It was the type of disorganisation you might attribute to genius. When Martin dropped papers or borrowed pens – he rarely returned them – you somehow felt that pearls were landing at your feet. Picking them up and handing them back – flyers for a forthcoming rally at Town Hall square, press releases for a visiting activist, never course notes or journal articles – you felt enriched, briefly. Your pen would at least be conscripted into the service of a worthy cause.

Dove was indeed at that moment groping through her bag for a Ball Pentel, her favourite type, to lend to Martin when she became aware of the younger man slipping into the booth, moving close beside her and pressing her against the wall. She felt his arm behind her and stiffened. He smiled. She found the pen, wishing she had a cheap biro instead, and handed it over, glancing at the man's face, side on. He seemed to have a pleasant smile.

'What are you doing later today?' he said.

Before she could answer he turned to Martin and asked him about that new member of parliament who'd said something inflammatory about the country being swamped by Asians.

'John Howard's encouraged that,' was all that Martin said, shaking his head. 'Fucking hell.'

She opened her mouth to reply, then shut it again. She was doing nothing later that day, or just doing the usual. Going home to the flat where she still lived with her mother, revising her notes (boring, nerdy) having dinner, watching *Friends*, the new show that everyone was excited about, which she tried to be. Her mother hated it. Instead, she would be reading. She was always reading. Tonight, if she hadn't already finished it while Dove was at university, it would be *Camille's Bread*, shortlisted for that year's Miles Franklin award. Jane had been telling Dove she should read it. It was set in Glebe for a start, and she was sure Dove would like it. It's about us, she said, ordinary inner city people, about relationships, and love and being a parent. Dove turned off at the mention of macrobiotic food but her mother's enthusiasm stayed with her. Jane always read the most up-to-date novels. She had already read through the highlights of the latest fiction listed for awards, what people were talking about. *Highways to a War*, she told Dove, was all about loss and moral values and it was admirable but it did not really do it for her like *Camille's Bread* did, which was about bread for a start: how amazing was that!

'Dove,' she said, 'don't you remember when you were a kid how much you liked white slices, how you'd pull them out of the bread bag just like Camille and eat them with no butter, no Vegemite, nothing?'

What a small thing. She couldn't imagine telling this man any of that. She knew what she was meant to say. Going to see *Cosi* or *Love and Other Catastrophes* at the Dendy cinema, or catching the latest Midnight Oil performance at the Revesby Workers' Club, an acceptably unreconstructed venue.

By the time the man had resumed his attention to her, Dove had decided.

'Going home and watching the news,' she said, getting up. 'I want to see what this Pauline Hanson woman is all about.' She thought his mouth dropped open as she moved away.

7

⸿ SHE MET RON AT CHURCH SOON AFTER returning home. She had not particularly planned to keep attending church, it was something they'd had to do every week at her Anglican school, but she kept it up out of habit, and for the welcome routine it provided. But an older woman had approached her one Sunday after morning prayer and grabbed her hands.

'You should come in the evenings,' she'd said. 'More fun for young people like you.'

And Ellis realised it would be a good way to make some friends her own age, now that her life had entered a whole new phase. Doing her secretarial certificate and looking for a part-time position in an office left little room for going out and meeting people.

It turned out that two of the woman's seemingly numerous children were involved, running the fellowship group and playing guitar. They met at seven-thirty in the church hall for an hour or so after church, and drank lemonade and weak coffee with biscuits while they sang folk songs or played records, and discussed Bible readings. Sometimes they went to the bowling alley on Saturday night, or to the movies. One of the members was, like her, an only child but with generous, hospitable parents who allowed the group access to their huge house, which had a pool and double garage. They sometimes gathered here, in the living room if Steve's parents went out, which they often did, or the recreation room adjacent to the garage where Steve had a number of musical instruments, a dartboard and even his own fridge.

Ron had joined the group several months before she had, along with his friend Philip, both of them having left a church in a neighbouring suburb. When asked why by various members of the youth group, Philip always responded firmly though non-specifically, indicating that their church had not been nearly so progressive as St John's, where the rector was happy to let the youth group take charge of the music for the evening service, and where the rector's wife, who was not much older than the members of the group, wore white lipstick and sometimes appeared at the evening services in pantsuits, to the outrage of some of the congregation.

They first talked together, alone, in the huge kitchen at Steve's place, having volunteered to take care of the coffee while the others finished listening to a program on the radio.

'Can you help me set out the cups?' she said. 'And find the sugar.'

'Yes, for sure.' He hunted around in the pantry and produced a sugar bowl and a packet of Scotch Finger biscuits.

'Should we open them?'

'Why not? There's plenty of food there. Looks like Steve's olds eat nothing but sweet biscuits.'

Away from Philip, he seemed more chatty, relaxed. Ellis noticed they did everything together, though Philip was at teachers' college and would soon be doing his two years' country service. Philip was a keen amateur photographer and was forever fiddling with lenses and coloured filters. If he didn't have his Canon around his neck it would not be far away, in his briefcase or in the car. Those celebrating twenty-firsts, and the couple of engagements within the group, had been presented with dozens of photographs of the event, where Philip had almost without their realising taken unofficial photos. When people, some who had not known him very long, offered to pay for the prints he always magnanimously brushed them aside, claiming he was glad to practise his skills, and besides Ron often developed them in his laboratory, after work. Ron had once mentioned to the group that Phil could have been a professional, if he wanted, but his friend had frowned and, it seemed to Ellis, shut him down.

Ron worked at the university as a laboratory assistant. After that first night in Steve's kitchen he began paying her special attention and if she suspected that Philip was somehow miffed, these suspicions were allayed when Philip – despite a dark and glowering sort of demeanour, one suggestive of strong tempers and inflexible views – extended his great and talkative wit towards her, almost pointedly, it seemed. Though the first few times he came upon Ellis and Ron talking together, in a corner of Steve's recreation room, or on the church porch after service, he stared then turned on his heel and found someone else to talk to or direct his camera at. But then he also went out of his way to be helpful to Ellis, offering lifts here and there if she needed them. One evening he appeared in his mother's Hillman Minx as she was walking down the steps of the technical college in Mary Ann Street.

'I'm here to drive you home,' he said. The passenger door was already open as if there were some sort of arrangement.

She was flattered, and disturbed, easing herself into the seat while trying to thank him as well as seek an explanation.

'Your boyfriend's busy.' He said it like Ron was an affliction, and she was demanding.

'I wasn't expecting him, actually.' She pushed aside the clutter of camera equipment on the floor of the car. 'He hardly ever picks me up.'

Philip ignored that. All the way he chatted nonstop about plans he and Ron had for a camping trip in the next holidays. She had the distinct feeling these plans were meant to convey something to her.

The next evening she asked Ron if he had put the idea to Philip to pick her up.

'And is it true you're going to the Kangaroo Valley in the summer break?' Not that she was proprietorial, just that she felt he should have mentioned it. But he only shook his head and smiled.

'That's Phil for you! Full of odd ideas.'

Philip made suggestions as to where she might get a job, gave advice on where she should shop for clothes (his three sisters had discovered all the bargain stories in town), and loaned her books on odd topics that from politeness she pretended interest in: a biography of John, the saint for whom their church was named, a book about religious icons. Along with his passion for photography, and his love of football and cricket, he had a strangely prodigious knowledge of church history, which to her seemed an odd thing in a geography teacher. All his interactions with her comprised a mixture of enthusiasm and even generosity but with an unmistakable disdain, as if she were a crippled relative whom his mother had ordered he be kind to. He never once betrayed a sense that there might have been something between Ellis and Ron, despite using the word boyfriend with special disdain.

*

AWAY FROM PHILIP, Ron was an insistent sort of man, and she became carried away by his infectious enthusiasm for fun.

Whether they were simply taking a walk around the park at night, chatting and joking, or sitting in the car twisting the radio dial this way and that, getting the latest hits, time spent with Ron was always something of an adventure.

He made her laugh. Besides, he had a job, he'd bought his own car, new, and was paying it off, and he'd already travelled. He'd been camping in New Zealand and had cruised around the Fiji islands with his family when he was sixteen, her age. And although he still lived with his parents, he and his brother shared a converted garage as a bedroom and boys' den. It was a place of late-night comings and goings with a radio left on most of the time. Eric always seemed to be going out just when they arrived back from church or a movie. There was an old lounge chair with its legs sawn down so it slumped in front of a second television, bought when Eric had turned twenty-one two years before. Ellis's father had only acquired his first television while she was away at boarding school. He spent long patient minutes before every program fiddling with its controls to get a good picture and by the time he was done she felt almost intrusive, asking to watch a show she wanted.

Most amazing of all in Ron and Eric's den was something called a lava lamp, which Ron's cousin had recently brought back from America, a dim lamp with orange-coloured water and blobs of pale wax. The first night he took her to his place, she was fixated by it. He held her close and turned her head to face him while he reached around and up her jumper. She watched the blobs that rose and fell with a slow hypnotic pace.

'Kiss me,' he murmured, feeling down her side, across her breasts, and down her waist, past her hips, before cupping her buttocks firmly.

Kiss him? She did not know how. And if she thought about it she would know even less.

He then turned all the lights off except for the lava lamp and pulled back the blankets for them to snuggle under in the chilly room. It was winter and she kept most of her clothes on. Before she realised it, they were not just playing around, as he'd done before a few times in the car, when he pushed his hands up under her skirt and past the band of her pants, another time when he had pressed her against the porch wall and released her breasts from her bra, at the same time placing her hand against his hard groin. She felt his fingers fumbling around, heard him sigh, close into her neck, then felt some great pressure between her legs, followed by a sudden warmth that could have been her own body or his. Despite what she had understood from all the talk at school, it didn't hurt at all. Even as it was over and Ron was groaning with his head on her chest and she could feel a dampness in her crotch, she was not entirely sure whether they had done it or not. Not until Ron raised his head and said, 'Are you okay?'

'Yes,' she said, 'I think so.' There didn't seem to be any blood, though she felt sodden with something.

'Sorry, maybe I shouldn't have done that.'

She pushed herself up in his bed and looked down on him, his hair flopping over his forehead.

'It's okay. It was all right.' *All right?* Why would she say that? Wasn't it meant to be the most amazing thing in the world?

'Your fault, though,' he said, reaching up to kiss her again. 'So damn sexy. I just couldn't help myself.'

Then he gave her a handkerchief and she cleaned herself and dressed, refusing to let him put on the overhead light. She retied her shoes by the glow of the lava lamp. A lump of wax in the shape of Casper the friendly ghost separated into two and rose to the top.

*

RON DROVE THE CAR slowly along the street until they were three houses before Ellis's, then cut the engine. VWs had such a distinctive tick-tick sound. Deceiving her father did not come easily, for she loved and respected him with equal devotion, but this wasn't the first time she'd stolen illicit time with Ron. As she was so late, she would have to walk down the side path to where the back door would be unlocked. Even though it was dark she knew her way, knew without needing to look when to avoid tripping on the raised crack in the path, knew to clear the corner downpipe without kicking it or stepping on the grate. Her father's light in the front room was off, she'd observed as they drove past. The screen door would not squeak if she opened it slowly enough, and then her bedroom was at the kitchen end of the hall. If her father did hear her she could always have just been going to the bathroom right next to it.

They sat in the dark looking ahead, Ellis twisting her hands in her lap while Ron drummed on the steering wheel with his fingertips. This time they'd not been to Ron's place, but had just been sitting in the car for ages after church. She could have walked home, it was only a few blocks, but he had insisted on driving her. If her father did know she wasn't coming straight home every Sunday, he had said nothing, seeing as having a daughter attend youth fellowship after the evening service was hardly cause for concern in anyone's book. If only he knew, Ellis thought, twisting her hands tighter. She realised they were trembling so she placed them under her armpits. Ron stiffened beside her.

'No need to be like that,' he said.

'Like what?' She turned to look at him but his face was in profile. He had an attractive straight nose and dark hair that flopped over his brows, which he was prone to pushing back in an unselfconscious gesture that she had found endearing right from the start.

'So aloof.'

'How do you expect me to be?' Now she felt a distinct wave of revulsion for him. Perhaps the strain echoed through her voice, but he turned and placed his hand over hers and pressed them firm.

'I'm sorry, Ellie. I'll sort something out, I promise.' He pulled her head towards him and laid it on his chest. She suppressed a sob, wishing she could believe him but doubting that he could ever sort this something out. Even her father never called her Ellie.

'I'd better go.'

The worst thing, thought Ellis, trying to make her hands stay still while he hummed in the dark, was that he had not really even been her boyfriend, despite Philip's occasional arid use of the word. They'd been seeing each other, that was true. But in the eight months or so, there had been no real date, no night alone at the movies, just the two of them. No quiet dinner at a restaurant somewhere. Nothing to mark out that what they were doing was somehow special, set apart from the rest of the group. She went along with him to fellowship events as if she were any of the other girls. At times in the movies if they were at the end of a row or behind the others, in the dark he would hold her hand and sometimes press it into his lap. He never, though, put his arm around her, only those few times they were alone at his place.

And he had never appeared at her front doorstep bearing a rose or an orchid, to shake hands with her father and promise to drive carefully and bring her home by ten-thirty. The rest of the young people in their group were aware that she and Ron had a thing going but that it was also casual. Had either of them disappeared, or had they simply not spoken to each other again, no one would have said a word. What she had realised – and now she knew this was not a sudden revelation but something that had been in the back of her mind all along – was that as

Ron and Philip had been friends since primary school, indeed neighbours until Philip had moved into rooms above a hotel near the teachers' college where he worked as a night manager, there was a bond between them; and that she, like any other young woman, was bound to be an interloper.

What Ron had just told her, however, after they left the fellowship meeting earlier that night, was somewhat more complicated than she could possibly have imagined. All she understood was that now she was as near enough to being on her own as she had ever been.

'We can still see each other,' Ron said as she got out of the car. It was almost as if he had done nothing wrong, nothing at all, and she nearly felt sorry for him except that already she felt the bitter taste of jealousy.

'No, we can't,' she said. But she closed rather than slammed the door of the VW.

*

SHE FILLED THE TUB and added bubbles from a pink bottle that had been on the shelf for years — she couldn't remember how long, or who had given it to her. They hardly ever had baths, her father having a thing about wasting water or soaking in your own dirt or something. She couldn't remember exactly what his objection was now, just that it was one of those things that had been there all her life. Lying there with the bubbles up to her chin she realised she seemed to have forgotten lots of things, and yet memories of other events were crystal sharp, stabbing her mind with a cruel clarity. Despite the fog in her head she saw every step she had taken that night a few months back, after she and Ron had made love properly, when his brother was out.

It had not even been very late. She'd been home by nine-thirty and had shared a cup of hot chocolate with her father before going to bed, as if everything were perfectly normal and she had not done the most foolish thing in the world, or had unwittingly changed the course of her life. She saw herself sitting there at the kitchen table, swirling the chocolate that had gone muddy in the bottom of her cup, and wondering how her father could stand there draining his own cup before tightening his dressing gown cord and kissing her goodnight. She wondered how he could possibly not know. Surely he would slam his cup down on the table and then accuse her. He would smell the odour of stolen virginity on her as he bent to kiss her on the forehead. Well after he had left the room her body had still been tense with the awful thrill of it. She forced herself to stand and rinse her cup at the sink before switching off the kitchen light. She'd had a long bath that night too.

Ellis now wondered how she could have fallen for Ron's clichés. Sexy. Damn sexy. Worse, thought them a compliment. And though she despised him for his weakness she knew it was not entirely his fault, and despised herself even more. But now it was clear there could be no future with Ron, she knew she could not afford to hold a grudge against him. She would not be guilty of that too. Despite the haze surrounding her in the past few weeks, she could see clearly now what needed to be done.

She pulled the plug in the bath, dried off and got into a clean nightgown before brushing her teeth. She spat vigorously into the basin, then cleaned them again before snapping off the light and going to her bedroom. She sat on the bed, hugging her knees and thinking, staring at the night-light in the shape of a fat crescent moon with a cartoonish cow jumping across it. It had sat on the bookshelf on the wall opposite for as long as she remembered. It was time to get rid of that light, she thought, before turning down the covers.

8

⸿ THE CAT CLIMBED RIGHT INTO HER LAP, his motorised purr vibrating gently through his whole body and into her hands. His eyes closed, his neat head nudged her stomach until she rubbed it again. The motor hummed louder. Was this normal? Perhaps she had better take Viv to the vet, today.

She could not even remember his name now, the man in the booth. Jared? Jason? A Greek or Hebrew name, something with a J, she thought. Not James. An unusual name. Martin would remember: she still saw him these days.

The man's smile had stretched wider than normal, and she'd noticed his teeth, small and gappy. His arm had tightened, and then she had felt his fingers stretching around to land on her right breast. No one else noticed. Most people were gone. Martin was sorting pages and Angela had sat down to fill up a fountain pen before her next lecture. Dove edged back, but there was no more room to slide away. Plus the pressure on her breast was so subtle, even she doubted it. Angela was talking to Martin about a film they had seen the night before.

'Distorted,' Martin said, not looking up from some pages he was marking. 'The guy always uses the camera like that.'

He shuffled the pages, caught a folder just before it fell, then slipped Dove's Ball Pentel into his top pocket and scratched his neck under his beard.

Nothing, surely, was amiss. Martin's glasses, stuck together at one joint with sticky tape, were slipping down his long nose as he leaned towards Angela, who was wiping the tip of her fountain pen with a tissue. Dove felt the hand, the whole hand now, squeeze her breast. Angela carefully replaced the cap on her bottle of ink – she had numerous stains on her fabric bag from past leakages. Dove pushed the man beside her at hip level and he just smiled again, then turned to face Martin.

'Did you see his first? Forget the name of it. They showed it at the film festival a few years ago.'

He squeezed her again. It was almost affectionate. Unbelievable: he was groping her while carrying on a conversation. But maybe it was her? Maybe there was nothing going on. Or maybe this was what adult sophisticated people did and she was stupid, middle-class and repressed, unliberated and prudish, and should be enjoying it. She squirmed, swallowing her distress. She thought she might gag with the effort of doing nothing. How had her face not turned red? How had neither Angela nor Martin noticed she was being violated?

'Are you going to hear Wandsworth speak later?' Martin had put down his armload of books and papers and was retying a sneaker lace, one foot up on the edge of the booth table.

Because perhaps it was not a violation. J yawned, pushed his hair back with his free hand, massaged her breast harder with the other.

'Nah. Heard him speak last week.'

Wandsworth was a famous visiting lecturer from New York. It was too casual. It was surreal. J, she knew, was their friend. She should shove him away and cry out. They would be puzzled, offended, hurt. J would continue smiling, holding his hands up as if to show how clean they were. He really had a soft, round face. Curls clustered around his forehead. You could use him as a model for Cupid. She would be considered a fool. How rude it would be to accuse their friend of groping her, if that's what it was. What a breach of good manners it would be to cry out, here in a public place, and protest that she was being mistreated so.

Or how laughable would it be, for her. Or even contemptible. That she wouldn't take advantage of a sexual invitation, that she wasn't grown-up enough, woman enough, to take it in her stride, to nudge him back, or wink and play along. What was wrong with her? Why on earth wouldn't she just accept the situation, and lick his ear or place her free hand straight onto his groin? How often was a girl given a chance like that?

As she countenanced her inability to find a way to react appropriately, at the same time she nevertheless registered the outrageousness of what was happening. It was as if she were divided down the middle by a dotted line. Tear here and you would have the free-spirited, good-humoured Dove, uninhibited by sexual and social mores, and here you had repressed, uptight, frigid Dove: which one would you toss aside? She wanted to be neither. She felt, though, there was no middle ground. All the while, this eternity of confusion, the lifetime of torment which she felt might define her forever, was a mere minute or two while Angela fussed with her bag and Martin said something about getting another coffee.

Later she would wonder if it was simply her incorrigible politeness, or if there was something more to it, if she were too passive, a willing victim. Was there something about her that invited people to violate her? Was she doomed to be walked over like this, treated as a thing? Later, too, she felt cold with anger and told herself that if it were happening all over again she would have no trouble in pouring the rest of her coffee over his lap, or biting him hard on the ear while feigning a reciprocal kiss. All she knew at the time was that she was incapable of anything but silent restraint. It seemed forever until Angela and Martin trailed away, asking her if she was coming too.

'Yes!' she almost shouted in relief. And J had no option but to stand and release her.

The next time she had spotted him he'd smiled again but she had taken a chair from one of the other tables and placed it safely at the edge of the booth.

*

SHE THREW THE DREGS of her coffee into the garden and eased the cat out of her lap. He stretched and walked off down the back steps. A visit to the vet would be a complete waste of time, she thought, not to mention money, for he seemed perfectly well. And then she was smitten by a stroke of pure guilt, like a hot knife had pierced her chest. Her mother would not have thought that. Whatever limited income she had, she would never have begrudged the cat his health check, just as she had never stinted on anything for Dove.

She walked after him, calling, 'Viv, Viv! Come on, Viv,' until she spotted him under a hibiscus bush, his dark grey coat camouflaged in the shade. He would be plotting the death of some small animal, no doubt, a fledgling or a harmless mouse. Cats, she knew, were incorrigible hunters, one reason she'd never wanted to have anything to do with them.

'Viv!' She crouched down and pushed her arms through the lower branches of the hibiscus. 'Come here, Viv.'

He was just out of reach right up against the fence, staring back implacably, his eyes cold grey pebbles, the irises dilating rapidly in the gloom like blots of ink. There were lizards along the fence, she remembered, tiny skinks that flickered in and out of the garden and along the path to the washing line. They would be no match for those sharp dainty claws. She crawled under the bush.

'Come here, you little bastard.'

He was still, his body sleek, compact, as composed as a pistol in its case. But just as she reached for his front legs, Viv shot past her and ran up the garden. By the time she crawled back out and brushed off her hair he was sitting at the back door, not a whisker moving.

The hot knife stabbed her again. Viv was an indoor creature, he would not have a clue how to kill anything. The most wildlife he had encountered had been the occasional cockroach, and even then Dove recalled him once half-heartedly batting at one on her mother's kitchen floor, before giving up all attempts to conceal his disdain for any other form of life and turning away. Viv was not, she now realised with yet more guilt, so much a threat to lizards or birds as a cat that was uncatlike. She wished she could like him more but this only made her feel sorry for him, even contemptuous.

Viv had spent his life in the second-floor flat that still awaited Dove's decision to move or sell. He had never stalked mice and the closest he had come to a bird was apprehensively sitting on the balcony of her mother's living room. It faced the front, a pleasant garden of palms and bougainvillea, and there was a stand of callistemon in the street where in the evening noise scraped from the rainbow lorikeets, an intense clamour like the sudden operation of dozens of rusty tools. Dove found them delightful and infuriating, just a few of them enough to make a racket, like their throats needed oiling, but their energy was thrilling. In the latter part of the day, when the first shadows of evening were being applied, they would descend like gleeful urchins and then depart in a mass, having picked clean the pockets of the blossoming trees. Viv, eyes swivelling, tail twitching at the tip, would not have stood a chance.

She opened the screen door and he darted inside ahead of her. She tipped cat biscuits onto a plate for him and filled his bowl with clean water. It was months since the funeral. She knew she should be thinking about her mother's things, and start clearing out her flat. She took her notebook and papers back to her desk in the front room. The young man in the booth, his name had been Jabe, she remembered. Jabez. Meaning 'cause of sorrow'.

9

⸦ SHE COULD NOT REMEMBER THE LAST
time she had seen Mrs Wood. The housekeeper had still come
and cleaned and cooked for her father while Ellis was away at
school, but during her holidays she rarely saw her. She knew she
lived several blocks down the road, in a small flat built before the
war. It was on the corner, a red brick building of six flats, with
a garden out the back and a side door through a paling fence
in the laneway, where not so long ago the nightsoil man had
emptied the pans. At the front, behind bevelled glass doors, was
a brown-carpeted foyer and a staircase with chrome handrails
that curved up to the first floor. A potted aspidistra stood on a
squat pedestal and as her eyes adjusted to the light she realised
she was not sure of the number. All these years and she had taken
the woman for granted, it seemed. She could not have asked her

father, who perhaps himself did not know anyway. Outside one of the ground-floor flats was a white wicker perambulator with a rumpled baby blanket and a knitted bonnet hanging from its handle. The door to the other flat still had a Christmas wreath on it and Ellis knew this could not be it either: Mrs Wood would never have allowed a decoration to be displayed so many months out of the season.

Upstairs, light streamed through a stairwell window showing the third and fourth flats. Behind the door of one she heard the chatter of a radio. She pressed close and heard the sound of a horserace being called. She knocked on the other door, to no response, and so climbed to the second floor, feeling a sudden wave of fatigue hit her with such violence she was forced to sit on the top stair and catch her breath. She felt hot and clammy. Her pulse seemed to be racing. It was as if she could hear the blood coursing through every vein in her body. When her heart stopped beating quite so loudly she rose and went and knocked at the first door, which opened almost at once, before she passed out.

*

'ARE YOU FEELING BETTER NOW?'
A wet cloth was peeled off Ellis's forehead and replaced with a fresh one. It was so cold that she briefly shivered. She looked

around. She was lying on a green velvet couch, her feet dangling over the edge. Mrs Wood sat in a chair beside her.

'Try and sit up.'

Ellis rose to a sitting position. She was facing a deep window, almost a doorway, which opened onto a balcony, past which she could see the tops of a row of palms.

'Thank you. Yes, I feel a bit better.'

Mrs Wood got up and went into the kitchen. Ellis heard the clink of porcelain, the rush of water, the rattle of spoons, and presently the woman returned with a cup of tea. She handed it over and sat down again without a word. Ellis took a sip and without meaning to pulled a face.

'Yes, with sugar. I know you don't take it but I'd say you need it.'

Ellis drank again then replaced the cup carefully in the saucer. It was pale green, the same plain design as the yellow ones in their household. She stared at the cup and saucer. The green was so much nicer than the yellow. It was a soft shade. The translucent reddish brown tea looked pretty in contrast to the colour. Leaves and bark. The colours of nature. Finally she lifted her eyes from the teacup to find the other woman staring at her. Then Mrs Wood went and took a packet of Ardath from the sideboard and lit a cigarette with a silver table lighter in the shape of an Egyptian pyramid and returned to her seat. Ellis found her face impossible to read. She stared at her cup again. How long since Mrs Wood had been around, since she had stopped working for them? Then she remembered.

'You don't drink tea.'

'No. Only coffee.' She drew on her cigarette and leaned back in her chair. Ellis felt her disinclination to talk most strongly. Clearly the woman was waiting for her. She drained her tea and replaced the cup, then looked her in the eyes.

'I need help. Please.'

Mrs Wood raised her eyebrows, drew a final mouthful of smoke deep into her lungs, leaned forward and butted the cigarette, then leaned back again, her leisurely movements suggesting she had this sort of conversation every day. She was dressed in the same clothes that Ellis always remembered her wearing: the short-sleeved sweater of a twin set, a grey pencil skirt, and brown lace-up brogues with a modest heel. Dressed like this, she could be doing anything from housekeeping to office work, though Ellis assumed she was still working for the council. Part-time work perhaps, seeing as she was home so early on a weekday afternoon.

Finally, she spoke. 'What makes you think I can help?'

Ellis prickled. She hadn't meant to imply anything, anything at all. It was simply that she was so alone.

'I don't know anyone else,' she said quietly. 'I'm sorry.' Now, thought Ellis, was the moment she might have broken down and cried but she would not. She absolutely would not lose control. She would leave before she became visibly upset, or inadvertently insulted Mrs Wood any further. She did not understand how there seemed such a huge divide between them, why there was such reserve from the woman she remembered as being the only person approaching a substitute mother all her life. She looked around for her shoes, as Mrs Wood had evidently slipped them off when she laid her on the couch.

'No need to be sorry. It's just that . . .'

'Yes?'

The woman shook her head. 'No matter.' She nodded towards Ellis's stomach. 'What about you then? How long?'

'Nearly three months.'

'And you're certain?'

Her breasts had been so sore. She felt bloated all over. Her skin felt like it was on fire at times. And at other times, like today, she felt that thrumming in her ears, like the roar of her blood circulating. That was aside from the fact she had missed two periods. She was certain all right. She had felt sick with the knowledge of it for the past few weeks, though that could have been one of the signs anyway.

'And of course you can't tell Edgar.' It was a statement, not a question.

Her father's name sounded oddly tender and familiar in Mrs Wood's mouth. Now, with the reference to her father, she did not trust herself to speak, fearing she would break down. She shook her head.

'What about the boy? Or is he a man?' She sounded cynical.

'He's twenty. He said he would pay.'

Mrs Wood having been so passive now seemed hardly able to contain herself. She threw her arms out and sprung up from her chair, exasperated.

'Oh yes. Of course he will pay! Don't they always offer to *pay*.' She almost snorted at the idea, spitting out the last word as if it were poisonous. She paced over to the sideboard and took another cigarette, drawing back on it quickly then going to the window which she pushed up as high as it would go. She crossed her arms over her chest, raising a hand now and then to smoke quickly. From the couch Ellis could see her neat chest rising and falling with the effort of her indignation. Then she threw the butt into the garden and turned to face Ellis.

'It's just after five. Time for a gin and tonic.'

Ellis shook her head. Even if she did drink, the thought made her queasy.

'No, of course not,' Mrs Wood said more to herself. 'You're still only a child, really,' she murmured, going to the kitchen again and taking out the bottle of gin.

At their house, five in the afternoon, ritualistically, Mrs Wood had always made herself a gin and tonic. Sipping it slowly, she would roll pastry or run beans through the stringer, or shake a bottle of water with a perforated cap over the laundry, rolling it tight to keep it damp for ironing later in the evening. She only ever had the one drink, and replaced the bottle of Gordon's in the kitchen cupboard rather than the sideboard in the dining room where Ellis's father kept his bottles of brandy and whisky and the soda syphon.

'I'd better go.'

She rose and looked around for her shoes. They had been placed beside the sideboard. Ellis held onto it while fastening the straps of her shoes, then straightened up. There was a small silver-framed photo of a younger Mrs Wood and a man in uniform. He had a straight, serious mouth but there were laughter lines at the corners of his eyes. She was wearing a pale belted frock and was holding a small bunch of flowers with two ribbons trailing down to her hem. Her hair, which seemed fairer than now, had been curled and brushed back from her face. Her lips were very dark. Mrs Wood always wore her hair pulled back into a plain French roll, and pale pink lipstick.

'It was during the war,' she said, holding a cut-glass tumbler from which she took a sip. 'There was rationing of clothes and other things. It was hard to get material for wedding dresses.'

She placed the tumbler down and picked the photo up. Ellis noticed the clean line of her jaw, set firm. The precise shape of her mouth, which trembled slightly as she gazed at the photo. She wondered how old she was.

'What was his name?' Ellis had never heard her speak of any man, let alone a husband. But of course there must have been one.

She threw Ellis a glance as if considering what amount of information she ought to divulge, then sighed again.

'Frank.'

She placed the photo face down on the sideboard, and drank from her gin and tonic. Then she put the glass down abruptly, her face closed over and she steered Ellis to the front door.

'I'll walk down with you, make sure you're all right.'

Downstairs, light streamed into the foyer, making dust motes dance. The sweet tea had revived her but Ellis still felt leaden. After she got home she would have to cook dinner, not that she felt like eating. Fortunately she had already shelled the peas and trimmed the chops. She had read a recipe in the women's pages of the *Sun-Herald*, describing how to stuff lamb loin chops with a crumb and herb mix and secure them with toothpicks, and pan fry them instead of placing them under the griller. She would finish them off and get the potato au gratin out of the refrigerator, leftovers from two nights before which would have to do. Her father would be home soon, his appetite sharpened from a couple of after-work beers with the assistant bank manager.

'Do you know why I always have a gin and tonic at five?'

They were at the threshold of the building. Ellis shook her head.

'Frank loved his G and T. The few years we were together, we always had one at five. He made them for us.'

Ellis murmured. She wasn't sure where this reminiscence was going.

'My job was to keep a good supply of ice. Hard before we got a fridge. In the first place we lived, two rooms out the back of someone's house, there was only an icebox.' She looked directly at Ellis. 'Can you believe it? An icebox!' Though she was not laughing. Indeed she was looking quite grave and Ellis got the impression that Mrs Wood was telling her something of great importance, if only she could listen properly enough. 'And when

Frank was away with the army,' she went on, 'I would have a drink for both of us, because he couldn't.' She paused. 'And now I have one in his memory.'

Ellis nodded, unsure if there was anything she could or should say. Mrs Wood had her hand on the bevelled glass front door anyway, before she said goodbye, and Ellis realised that she had still not indicated if she could help her or not. But when she opened her mouth the strangest thing of all came flowing out, as if it were a genie from an uncorked bottle.

'Can you tell me what happened to my mother?'

But Mrs Wood was closing the door and had either not heard or would not say.

*

THREE DAYS LATER ELLIS was walking home from the main road. It was nearly ten pm. Her father had at first met her at the stop, but she had become used to the walk on her own, reassuring him that it was perfectly safe in the dark. Several other people from tech travelled on the crowded bus from Broadway to Parramatta Road, and the next bus she waited for at the start of Liverpool Road was always driven by the same friendly driver. It was well lit and had a dozen passengers, who all bonded in the late-night adventure of it; only once or twice there appeared a man who had somehow kept drinking after closing time, and even then the sort of things men like this said were more annoying than alarming. By the time she got to her stop she was in familiar territory.

The five-minute walk was something she normally looked forward to, though this night she felt strongly the leaden sensation that had overcome her entire body from time to time in the last couple of weeks, no matter how much she slept or rested. She had felt so tired. The last half-hour of Miss Allman's lesson had passed in a torment of stifled yawns and surreptitious eye rubbing. As soon as she got inside and had spoken to her father she would be heading straight for bed. Normally they sat over a cup of tea or hot chocolate while she ate some toast or a slice of fruitcake. He usually remembered to put the kettle on for them a few minutes before she walked through the door.

The lively evening air smelled strongly of mock orange blossom. The days were becoming warmer though the nights could get cool, and she wore her royal blue belted cardigan, the one she had knitted herself and adorned with silver buttons. She could also still smell the summery scent of cut grass from when the next-door neighbour had trimmed the front lawn that afternoon. The scent pulled at her memories, stirring something that emerged no more clearly than a formless sadness, a yearning for something undefined, just out of reach.

At her front gate a shape appeared.

'I thought it best to wait here for you.' Mrs Wood nodded towards the house in which sat Ellis's father and all the unspeakable consequences of knowing what was happening. She pressed a piece of paper into her hand. 'And please don't think this sort of information comes easily to me,' she said, almost hissing the words, she was speaking that low.

'Thank you.'

Mrs Wood turned to walk away but then an afterthought made her stop and face Ellis again. 'This young man. You're sure he'll pay? Because it's not going to be cheap.'

She thought for a moment, about the last time she saw Ron, how awful it was. There was not even the hope that she could marry him and sort it out that way, if she had wanted to. But she hadn't. She didn't want to marry him. She didn't want her life together with him, with any man, to be tainted like that right from the start.

'Yes, he'll pay,' she said. He would pay.

And although Mrs Wood was already walking off, Ellis thought she heard the faint words, 'Good luck,' wafting back on the breeze along with the scent of mock orange and cut grass.

I O

———

NOW IS THE TIME FOR ALL GOOD WOMEN to come to the aid of the party. The quick brown fox jumps over the lazy dog.

Dove typed the lines three more times, then took a sip of her wine. Her laptop was on the bar and this time of the day, early afternoon, the place was empty apart from her and Martin, who periodically disappeared outside to smoke. The bar was called Passageway for good reason. It was barely more than a hall, with a line of stools against the bar leaving just enough room to squeeze past to the back of the premises, down a step to the toilets, then along a hallway, even narrower, and down another two steps to a courtyard.

'Another?' She was drinking shiraz and Martin took her empty glass and held it up.

She wondered whether to order another, if that might mean the rest of the day would be a write-off. On a whim earlier in the afternoon she had left the house and walked up to the main street. Since giving up work, she had realised just that morning, she was in risk of becoming a hermit.

'No. I might go home and play music for the cat.' Lately, she had barely even spoken to the cat.

Martin poured her one anyway. 'On the house.'

Coming to Passageway was logical. It was close by, served good drinks, was quiet and she could catch up with Martin, if he was in the mood for a chat. Since their university days, nearly twenty years before, Martin had not become a politician or head of a powerful union or someone important at the ABC, as suggested by his intellectual reach and his many political activities. Nor had he finished his architecture degree either, but had started and abandoned yet another – law – before working in a series of short-term jobs. Research assistant to the Honourable Gough Whitlam, speech writer for a federal parliamentarian, editor of an arts journal that burned bright and fizzled out within eighteen months, deputy director of a charity that sent teachers to Africa, and more positions that Dove had forgotten. All his jobs ended prematurely though amicably as Martin's restless spirit moved on. He opened Passageway when his elderly father died and left him a small legacy, and as far as Dove recalled, the three years he'd been here were the most consistent in his life. It appeared that a bar was the perfect milieu for Martin's expansive mind and anecdotal wit, although despite being talkative and opinionated, he also knew when to stay quiet.

And he played excellent music, not too loudly. He was pausing the iPad playlist behind the bar now. He slotted a CD into the old player and turned around.

'What do you think of this? Maybe Viv would like it.'

She listened carefully, but could not identify it. She had no ear for music, despite all Jane's efforts.

'What is it?' It was wild, slightly off key, with lots of strings. 'Turkish music.'

It had taken her a long time after her mother died to work out that Viv was missing one vital element from his life, so she started playing him classical music. At first she could not bear to listen to the works her mother had been so skilled at playing and opted instead for safe, predictable, pieces. *Four Seasons*, of course. Sibelius's *Violin Concerto*. As soon as she got the sound level right the cat seemed happy, though this had taken a while. She first fiddled with the sound and tone and he growled and fretted and scampered around the house until she worked out that playing the music quite loudly in a room but with the door shut was perfect for him. This must have been how her mother played, loud but hidden away.

In the flat her mother always kept her violin and music stand in the spare room, and for some reason now the thought of her mother playing alone in that small room with the door shut, perhaps with the cat waiting outside the door, filled her with more sadness than anything else. She felt sadder than when her mother died, sadder than at the funeral, embarrassingly small though that was. Apart from Dove, her mother had died alone and the funeral was attended by a handful of friends, mostly distant, and a few relatives with whom, Dove knew, her mother only kept in touch at Christmas time out of a sense of duty. At the funeral, the organisation of which she had handed over entirely to the White Ladies, her mother's wish, she only began to have a sense of the disconnect of her mother's life. That Dove's own life was largely disconnected was not a revelation to her: Jane had always been open about the adoption and to Dove it was normal. And as for the rest, it was largely her choice, and mostly something she had lived with all her life, the knowledge of her outsider status. To her that was normal too.

But sitting in the tiny chapel at the crematorium, glancing at the few pews dotted with distant relatives and friends, all grey and pastel coloured, it struck her that there might have been a pattern in her life and her mother's life, and that her mother also had great holes in her existence of which Dove had been barely aware. She realised she should have asked more questions about the exact relationship, say, between the people she called Uncle Graham and Aunty Rose, and herself: perhaps they were not her mother's real uncle and aunt either, but close family friends. They had just always been there, and it had not occurred to her until this moment to question how they had got there. Long ago neighbours, perhaps. Or cousins several times removed. But it was too late to disturb the smooth, even tracks on which her small family's modest train had run for all these years, too late to disrupt the polite means by which they had all communicated for all her life. A funeral was not the time to ask, Excuse me, Uncle Graham, but how exactly do I know you? The funeral had ended with a recording of Bach's *Chaconne*, a piece Jane had favoured for its stately controlled passion, which continued to play as the coffin disappeared behind the red velvet curtains.

The sadness of thinking about her mother playing to the cat behind a closed door for all those years would not go away.

'I like it,' she said to Martin, gesturing to the CD player. The Turkish music was haunting and plangent. It contained strains of something almost familiar but out of reach.

Martin nodded, reaching for glasses. The bar was beginning to fill up. She decided to finish her drink then go home before succumbing to tipsy emotions. She typed another line.

When she first studied art she had no intention of doing anything more than something creative that would also please her mother's desire for her to become qualified, but it had hit her, even before Jane had become ill, how much she was unsuited to graphic design. She hated the manic pace of her job, the fact that she seemed to be the oldest person in the company by more than ten years, that she was obliged to turn out glib commercial work, the fact that she was not particularly talented anyway. She discovered she was good with colours but not with shapes. Or some jobs inspired her in the fine details, but she found it hard to concentrate on the overall concept. Her creative director had hinted they had lost a few clients because of Dove's failure to meet deadlines. It wasn't just that her mother was sick for months and she'd needed time off: she was tired of it all, tired of wringing out some perkiness, some fun, some cartoonish approach for clients trying to sell laundry products or vodka lolly drinks or street festivals.

For fun she changed the font in the last line she typed. It was not writing but it was doing something like it. If she performed enough of these exercises maybe real sentences would grow. Writing her story was more frustrating than she could ever have imagined, although she had not really imagined it: writing had leaped upon her unawares, from out of the dark, its claws unsheathed. But maybe she should not have given up work after all, or instead kept going part time. Mute grief, she suspected, was rendering her incapable of any productive work. Dove and her mother had been fond but independent, and even though they were both single, there had never been any question of them living together. After she had recovered entirely from that first stroke, Jane had still been able to cook, and clean, and do her washing and, with Dove's help, she coped. In fact it was not even a question of coping. She managed very well, and if Dove had not been around she would simply have bought her groceries online and caught taxis to her appointments. She had long given up her car to Dove anyway, asserting she never liked driving and didn't need it anyway, the flat being so close to the station. Dove for her part drove infrequently too, however as she was younger it was understood that she might have been more of a free spirit than her mother and would want to get out a lot more.

Sitting in front of her laptop in Passageway, now squeezed on either side by after-work drinkers, Dove was struck by how unlike a free spirit she was. Now that her mother was dead and there was no reason for her not to travel, to go anywhere she liked, or stay out all night, or bury herself under her bedcovers and not answer the phone for a week if she wanted, she found she had no desire to be free. Coming to have a quiet drink with Martin now and then was the most adventurous thing she could do. Her life struck her as unbearably sad. Pathetic, even. But probably that was just the second glass of shiraz. She should go home.

Standing on the footpath outside the bar she decided she would go back to her mother's flat, first thing the next day. She had been avoiding it, though telling herself that there was no pressure to clear it out and settle her mother's affairs. But equally there was no reason not to, now. And as tidy as the place was, she knew it would still be a big job. That sort of thing always was.

'Hey!' Martin emerged from the bar holding out the Turkish music CD. 'Take it. Play it to Viv,' he said and rushed back inside.

*

SHE TOOK THE CAT WITH HER, careful not to open the pet carrier until she closed the front door. He poured out of the basket like a bowl of oil, then slinked up the hallway and into the lounge room. After gliding around the room he came to sit quite still at the French doors. He closed his eyes and licked his paws.

The place did not smell as stale as she'd anticipated. But she took a few steps across the living room to open the French doors anyway, to let in the air. The tiny balcony contained one wooden chair and table, where an amber pressed-glass ashtray still held two silver butts. Her mother's one small indulgence, the occasional Sobranie cigarette while having a glass of wine of an evening.

On the tiled floor of the balcony was a row of black pots with dark brown stalks. Dove felt a spurt of guilt, until she remembered they would have died anyway. Her mother had a magic touch with maidenhair ferns, and it had become almost a joke: whenever she'd gone away and it had been up to Dove to care for them, the ferns had died, no matter that Jane went away for a weekend or a fortnight. Her mother had tried putting them in the bath where Dove only had to spray them with the shower. She had placed them on special absorbent mats to keep their roots cool. She had inserted slow-release water dispensers, which she made from plastic water bottles plugged with rubber stoppers. All methods had failed and Dove had regularly replaced the plants from the local nursery. During her first few weeks in hospital, before she deteriorated to the point where she could no longer talk, her mother had reminded her about the maidenhairs, and Dove had promised to check and water them. Indeed she had, once or twice, but she now remembered that just around the time her mother's condition turned, to the point where she had begun phoning nursing homes, the plants had started to demonstrate signs of stress.

She'd found her mother, after the second crippling stroke, lying immobile on the floor, and organised the ambulance, and spent most of the night at the hospital until she was settled and there was nothing else she could do for the moment. After that she'd returned to the flat to fetch Viv. She had packed his food and bowls and disposed of the litter tray, and locked him in the pet carrier then closed all the windows and fastened and bolted the French doors on the balcony – her mother, a fresh air fiend, and living on the second floor, always left windows open – when she'd noticed the row of ferns. She had unlocked the doors and fetched the plastic jug from the kitchen and doused them all in water as quickly as she could before locking the doors once more, all the while as Viv wailed piteously from his carrier by the door. She had only managed to visit the flat twice again since then, once to fetch the copy of *Wuthering Heights* Jane had requested, and during all those weeks when she had sat and read the novel to her mother, the thought of the maidenhairs had crossed her mind once or twice. But she hadn't had the time or the energy or maybe the interest to go and check on them, especially when in her mind the plants were doomed anyway.

She passed her hand across the stalks. The dusty remains of tiny leaves fell onto the balcony to join those dropped in the last months. The garbage bags were in the bottom drawer of the kitchen. She went over, took one out, and went back to the balcony, grasping the first of the dead plants and lifting it free of the pot. She paused, watching the dry dirt trickle to the concrete floor, then she replaced it and swiftly dropped all three pots into the garbage bag. The pots were only small. And she would never replant them with anything else.

She picked up a butt from the ashtray. It held a faint imprint of lipstick. Max Factor's Classic Coral: Jane had never worn any other. Even living alone, in the evening, she always wore lipstick. Dove emptied the ashtray into the bag then took it to the kitchen sink. Placing the bag by the front door to take downstairs later, she returned to the kitchen for the dustpan and broom.

Quickly, she decided what she had to do. Take each room one at a time. The bedroom would be the most difficult so she would tackle that first. But going in there and boldly opening wide the wardrobe doors she realised it would not be that hard at all. Jane was much shorter and smaller than she, so there was no question of keeping any of her clothes. She took from her bottom drawer in the wardrobe a silk Liberty print shawl, in rich dark reds and midnight blue, that Jane had had for as long as Dove could remember. She took the camphorwood jewellery box that held some jet beads with matching earrings, several rose gold chains, and Dove's baby charm bracelet. She already had Jane's watch and rings, which had been on her when she first went to hospital. From the spare room she took the violin and stood it by the door. Jane had lived her small neat life as if every day she were preparing for death. When she'd moved into this flat, she had cleared out all the clutter of her life. She'd bought new linen, new crockery, all minimal and spare, got rid of most of her appliances and kitchen clutter. 'Am I ever going to use this again?' She'd held up the waffle maker. They'd both laughed. Dove had pestered her for it when she was about twelve, and they had used it once.

Nothing was out of place, everything had been filed or disposed of or put away, and the only outstanding mail was what Dove herself had neglected in the last few months. She'd already had the phone, the internet, and the gas disconnected, and the electricity would go when she finished the cleaning. She would return with boxes for the books and the CDs. Everything else she would place in bags for a charity, St Vincent de Paul or the Smith Family. They could come for the clothes, the linen – only two sets of sheets and towels, nothing extraneous – and take the furniture, the modest serviceable kitchenware – she thought Jane had got it from Ikea – everything. When that was done she could set about selling the place. And then she could get back to her story.

By the time she was done Viv was waiting by his carrier at the front door, composed and purring. She thought it might have unnerved him, but it had been the right thing to do, bringing him back.

I I

————

❦ SHE MADE THE PHONE CALL FROM THE
telephone booth outside the corner grocery store, two blocks
up from her house towards the main road. She imagined the
grocer and his wife, who'd known her all her life, peering out
through the dim recess of their shop and watching her every
move, dropping sixpence into the slot, slipping Mrs Wood's piece
of paper out of her pocket. She imagined they knew that sweat
was pouring down her armpits, soaking her blouse under her
cardigan, that they could lip-read or perhaps even hear every
word of her conversation.

The woman at the other end of the line sounded young and
was unexpectedly friendly. She gave Ellis an address at the corner
of two streets in the eastern side of the city past Central Station,
and told her to wait there. It would cost somewhere between

fifty and eighty pounds, depending, the woman said, and Ellis did not dare ask depending on what.

On the day, she skipped classes and waited up the street for Ron to pick her up after work. He dropped her off right on time, six pm.

'Are you sure you don't want me to come? I will, you know.'

'They told me no one else. To come on my own.' She was rigid with apprehension, sitting in the car and trying to calm herself.

He got out, came around and opened the door for her, and helped her out. A brisk wind whipped her skirt around her legs as she got out of the car. Leaves and lunch papers scooted past on the footpath, and a sheet of newspaper clung to her ankle as she pulled her jacket closer. Kicking it free, she felt dishevelled and dirty already.

'It will be better if you just go, Ron.' She avoided his kiss, and felt worse about that as soon as he drove off, the tick-tick noise of the VW fading as he disappeared around the corner.

Ellis was anxious that too many people would still be about, that she would be recognised by someone, although it was many blocks away from the technical college down off Broadway and in an area where she knew no one at all and where she normally never came. But it was quiet by then, most of the offices having closed at five. The workers from the garment factories had knocked off long before. She checked her wristwatch, walked a few yards up the street, then back again. Within two minutes a large black car pulled up and a man wound the window down, calling out her name. He waved her into the back seat where another man sat holding a black scarf. Was that a blindfold? Ellis started to panic, feeling that the friendly woman on the phone had been a fraud. Both of them were wearing hats. Then the driver turned around and told the other not to worry, that it would be dark soon enough.

'Do you know where you are?' he asked.

'No.' Her mouth was dry, the word came out like a whimper. She cleared her throat and spoke again, feigning confidence. 'No, I don't. This is the other side of the city I'm used to.'

The man on her right asked her if she'd brought the money. She opened her handbag. Ron had given her eighty pounds, just in case, and she'd put fifty into an envelope, which she handed over to the man. He counted the notes then slipped them into his breast pocket, nodding. Then she turned away from him and stared out the window, seeing nothing. They drove for what seemed like hours, though it couldn't have been more than thirty minutes, then pulled up in a suburban street, high up. Treeless and exposed. She had the sense that they were very close to the water and only later on guessed it must have been somewhere in Bondi, or perhaps Dover Heights. The house was one of a duplex, and by now it was dark and there were no lights outside the place. The man who had sat beside her ushered her down a narrow side passage and then into a small room with a bare lino floor and two chairs. If it had contained a table with out-of-date magazines and a pot plant it could have been the ordinary waiting room of a suburban doctor.

He disappeared briefly through a door, returning with a glass of water.

'Here, take this.' He handed her a pill, which she took and swallowed. 'Now just wait. It won't be long.' He had taken off his hat and coat, and she realised he was completely bald, wearing thick horn-rimmed spectacles. He disappeared again, and as she sat there she began to feel cold. She heard muffled noises from inside, a door banging once, then again, low voices. By the time the man returned she was shivering uncontrollably. He showed her into the adjoining room where there was only a narrow high bed and a hospital screen. Another man, this time in white with strange white-blond hair, was standing at a corner table with a tray of instruments, and a woman who must have been a nurse, also in white, approached her.

'Just take your underclothes off, dear. Behind the screen.' Ellis fumbled with her clothes, her hands trembling as she removed her stockings and underpants. Then the woman helped her onto the bed and covered her with a sheet, pushing her skirt up to her waist. Despite the water she had sipped with the pill her mouth was dryer than it had ever been, her tongue unable to move. She could see herself as if she were watching from some distance and wanted to help herself and say something, anything, but could not move or speak to save her life. What was the pill they had given her, which she had swallowed without question? She now felt very thirsty, but her tongue seemed to have gone completely rigid. She thought of her father, whom she would perhaps never see again, and how he would wonder for the rest of his life what had happened to her, for she had no identification on her, and she knew, young as she was, that if anything went wrong with this operation she would be abandoned by these nameless people, whom she hoped against all hope were medical people, and her body would be left here to rot in this soulless, empty room. And Ron would be waiting at the designated spot at nine pm exactly to pick her up again and take her home and would be watching the time, wondering what to do. Would he go to the police and tell all, or would he go home and lie back on his bed and watch the wax slowly swell and bubble up and down the orange lava lamp?

The man and the woman – doctor and nurse, she begged mutely, please be a doctor and a nurse – now both put on masks and rubber gloves. Terrified as she was, she was glad to see that. When the doctor brought the pad soaked in ether to her face she was panicking to such an extent that she was frozen, and could not have cried or yelled out or even whispered a word to save her life. Her body twitched, her eyes swivelling in fear.

The woman spoke kindly to her. 'Just relax, dear, and breathe slowly.'

So Ellis forced open her mouth and gulped in air again and again, until she finally did relax as the pad was pressed over her mouth. It smells like nail polish remover, she thought, and that was the last thing she thought.

*

SHE WAS AWAKE, and could feel something like a towel between her legs. The nurse told her to sit up and brought a green enamel bucket, into which she promptly vomited. Her mouth despite this felt dry and she was still terribly thirsty.

'Have you brought some Modess?' Ellis nodded towards her handbag and the nurse handed it to her, then left the room while she dressed. She wished she had water to rinse her mouth but for some reason was unable to ask the nurse. She fumbled with her clothes, with the belt for the sanitary pads that stuck awkwardly between her legs; she put in two, just to be safe. Shivering still, she pulled her coat tighter as she sat once more in the waiting room. Finally the man reappeared, his hat and coat now back on, to take her outside, up the dark narrow path and to the car where the driver waited. All the way back to the city she tasted the acid of her own vomit. They were early, it was ten to nine, but Ron was there, leaning against the VW. She swayed out of the black car and across the kerb as he dashed over to catch her. He helped her into the seat and pulled the door shut. The men in the black car had already left.

'I'm okay,' she said. 'Just get me home.' She closed her eyes and ignored him, his questions: was it painful, did they treat her properly, would she be all right? After a few minutes she opened her eyes, groped in her handbag and drew out the remaining thirty pounds. 'Here. They didn't rip you off, at least.'

Pausing at a set of traffic lights, he looked at her, and she at him. He held his hand out to take the money, then withdrew it. The lights changed to green and he shifted gear.

'You keep it. Please.'

She shook her head, placed the notes in the glove box and closed her eyes again.

How she managed to walk unaided down the path and in through her front door she never knew. She looked in on her father, who was reading in the front room under the standard lamp, and murmured something about women's pains and needing to go straight to bed, then crept down the hall to the bathroom where she drank deeply from the tap. Then she fell into her own bed and an unbroken sleep.

The next morning she had to change her sheets, there was so much blood. The cramps were far worse than she'd ever experienced but she remained still for as long as she could with a hot water bottle, taking Bex like she'd been told, and by the next day the pain had gone away and by the day after the bleeding had stopped.

12

⁅ DOVE SAW A WOMAN IN A LONG SKIRT
striding across a dark landscape. It was not snowing, though
maybe it would be in another month. It was still autumn,
though very cold. The woman walked past the last of her father's
crop of beans, the leaves already turning brown. The beans
themselves would be tough but there might be another meal or
two from them. The sky was still and dark grey. Up this high, no
impediment of rock or tree between the ground and the earth,
the sky looked close enough to touch. On bright days it looked so
brittle you could almost punch through to heaven. This morning
the sky was elusive, with only a hint of light loitering over the
rise to her right.

The woman stepped over the low dry-stone wall and onto
the path of crushed pebble and slate, a half-hearted thing that

trickled across the next field, its boundary marked by a hedge of furze nibbled down by sheep. She stepped over this too, hitching her grey wool skirt, then dropping it again to keep striding across the knobbly hill that was littered with flat wet stones. Underfoot it was slick and icy, even through her boots. She'd brought her father's trowel, the one he kept for tending the beans, sometimes cabbages and parsnips, which were all that would grow in the windy patch behind the house. He should have kept a kitchen garden in the graveyard next door to the church, where there was more shelter, not to mention all those nutrients.

She felt the crunch of heather underfoot, a few sprigs someone had collected earlier and then dropped. She bent and gathered them up. That someone may even have been her. It must have been, for who else was there? She fingered their spiky buds, the tight little heads. Faded purple. Not quite purple: creamy pink. There was a faint scent still. She tucked them into her pocket and kept walking, bundling her shawl tighter, a thick one that she had knitted herself, though it was still not nearly protection enough with the wind snapping like a rabid dog.

She had made sure that Keeper remained on his chain, as he would only be a nuisance now. Today she did not want his rough comfort, the nudge of his nose against her skirt. That look in his eye. How dogs managed to judge by the faintest turn of their eyeballs, with just enough white to show that they knew what you were doing, or were thinking of doing. A sniff. Raising their muzzle then replacing it on their paws a quarter inch to the left or the right. Sighing. Then glancing again, displaying another sliver of white.

No, she wouldn't have it. Keeper had whined then settled down again on his sack beside the kitchen door. She'd given him a scone left over from yesterday's tea. Not hungry herself.

Over the next rise the pebble and slate path gave way to a thin track flattened into the grasses by years of walks, easy to follow in full daylight, but by then she would be returning. To either side the landscape vanished into the gloom, flat grey stones and stubbly tufts of grass and hillocks embraced by bracken that was so dark green it looked black, looming and receding as she continued her walk, head down, arms tightly held around herself. There to her left was the stand of stones, three enormous charcoal grey ones, piled together. A giant's pile: two large, with a smaller on top. Three potatoes set to the side of a plate. Three pears or apples in a bowl. Three dumplings. A gravy of green moss down the western side of the bottom two.

She shook her head, clearing her mind. Stay focused. The walk there and back took most people three hours, but she could normally do it in two with her long strides. Another reason she preferred to walk out on her own: no one else could ever keep up. To her right a faint brush of lighter grey, hinting at the dawn. And then another pile of stones, this time surrounded by crumbs of rocks. How they got there was anyone's guess. There were no mountains nearby to fall down, no cliffs to break off and tumble down to land and settle. This was the mountain, up here, this was as high as it could get. It was as if a heavenly being had opened up the skies and flung out a scuttle load of rocks onto the earth. The hill sloped down again soon, after the dumpling-pear-potato rocks. Up here, the landscape was immutable. It embraced her and propelled her along, up and down the rise where there was no other living creature but the wild wolf force that gnashed and howled in never-ending fury.

In the end it was always the wind that sent her home. Everything else, the vast bare immensity of the stripped land that met the unclothed sky, she could lose herself in, forever. Her cheeks were permanently stained red now, from a lifetime of the biting wind, her lips cracked and white.

Not even the cold itself bothered her. When the wind stilled, no matter how frozen the world, the cold was something she learned to embrace, though now she tucked the trowel into her sleeve and pulled the shawl closer over the bundle, bending her head against the fury screaming around her head. Her ears burned. She should have worn a bonnet instead of the shawl which she had pulled over her head, not that it would have helped that much. Useless things, bonnets. Sometimes she wore her father's old leather hat, when no one else was around to care. She almost laughed. No one else was around. It was just her, the cold earth deep below, the sky pressing down.

She crossed the waterfall as the eastern light was glinting on the rocks and the wind was dropping, as if to convince the dawn it had been asleep and tame all through the cold night. Further up she disturbed a family of plovers sheltering in a nest of heather, the muffled slapping of their wings briefly cutting across the silence. By the time she reached Top Withens, morning had properly arrived. One black-faced sheep trotted across her path, barely pausing to throw a lugubrious glance her way. She strode up the track straight behind the ruined house where two gaunt thorn trees stretched their limbs, as if craving alms of the sun.

*

DOVE SAT UPRIGHT. She looked at the pen which had fallen on the blanket, the purple notebook in which she hadn't written for ages but which she still kept on the bedside table. She had no idea if she had been asleep and dreaming, or writing in some sort of trance. But there were the words on the page beside her, the final ones in her own handwriting those of Emily Brontë herself. Either she was still dreaming, or she truly had been writing in her sleep. Or she was going mad.

Certainly her heart was beating like mad. She had never been to Haworth, never walked across those fabled moors behind the parsonage. But she felt chilled to the marrow, as cold as Emily herself out on that lonely walk in the early hours of the morning. And the scene had not finished writing itself. Now she was outside the scene rather than right there in it but it was as lucid as before, perhaps even more so. Indeed as she watched what the author of *Wuthering Heights* did next she felt that the clarity might be too painful to bear. Emily unwrapped her shawl and flung it on the yellow grass beside her. She took out the trowel and a small parcel, something wrapped in calico. She commenced digging beside the thorn trees where a clump of blue columbines was still in bloom, their heads dancing like bells. She eased them aside and began scraping away into the mossy turf, then jabbing into the damp earth. A few inches down and the soil became stony, for the whole place was on a knoll, the ruins of the house like an extension of the natural boulders tossed around it. Emily leaned back on her heels and wiped the back of her hand across her forehead then over the smooth brown hair, gathered into a tight knot.

She was left-handed, Dove noticed, but she passed the trowel to her other hand to keep attacking the soil, striking it deeper and deeper until it disappeared below the surface of the earth. She swapped hands again, leaning further forward then lifting the trowel up to drop the soil into a neat pile. Finally she laid the trowel down and picked up the parcel. Dove paid very close attention but could not discern what it might be. It was small and flat, but wrapped in layers to disguise the shape. Emily raised it to her chest and held it there for a moment with her eyes closed, then leaned closer and, in a slow and gentle manner, in contrast to her near frenzied digging, laid the precious thing in the hole she had made. Then she looked around, as if expecting there might be a witness, though who might possibly appear on this bleak early morning in late autumn, Dove could not imagine.

Quickly she replaced the soil, scraping it across with the trowel, then scattered pebbles and pulled at the spongy moss to cover the spot. In moments it was all done and she was slapping her hands to remove traces of dirt, then rising from her knees with the shawl and the trowel. As she began to walk away the wind picked up again, and she turned and faced the tiny grave, for there was no other word for it, and stood with her head bowed, pulling the shawl tight over her head. As an afterthought, she bent and plucked a few of the columbines, then she turned to walk back down the hill to the south. Before she disappeared, Dove heard for the first time something other than the whistling of the wind in the two lonely thorn trees: she heard Emily Brontë cough.

13

⟨ THE PHOTOS BURNED FASTER THAN SHE imagined they would. Perhaps it was the chemicals. Ron would know, with his scientific expertise, but she would never ask him that now, nor any other question, for she certainly would not speak to him again. A flame licked at the last corner, swallowed it, then vanished. She poked the ashes with the toe of her shoe. It had been a small fire, down the bottom of the garden under the plane trees, and only six photos, all postcard size but large enough. She pushed the dirt over the ashes, holding a hand to her chest where her breathing was strangely laboured. A few grey flakes remained.

She went over to the shed where the garden tools were propped against the far wall. There her father's thick wooden workbench, so aged and scored with marks it was black with time, its provenance impossible to guess. Perhaps an old chopping block. Or something he might have fashioned himself out of old railway sleepers or discarded fencing posts. He always kept it clear except for the massive vice, and although the shed was cluttered it displayed a pleasing order. Above the bench was a masonite board painted a dull cream, on which hung his collection of hand tools, their shapes outlined in indelible pencil. Some of them were missing now: the hacksaw, its bread-loaf shape clearly visible, and two of the set of five files which she remembered he had loaned to a mate a few years ago, though he had stopped complaining about their failure to be returned. Her father rarely used his tools now and only entered the shed to fetch the larger gardening implements and the rotary mower. He kept his secateurs and trowel and garden twine in an old wicker basket under the table on the back verandah. When she was younger Ellis remembered him spending hours down here, even during her school holidays, only emerging when the daylight through the tiny windowpanes, always festooned with cobwebs inside and out, faded to make work impossible. There was no electricity, and he had never installed a light.

The shed was dark now, in the late afternoon, as the windows were all but covered in ivy and the plane trees loomed even closer and denser than when she was a child. It seemed like a long time ago, but when she thought about it, it was really only four or five years since her father had stopped making toys and small pieces of furniture for the house and odd things for

Mrs Wood. He had made a set of wooden alphabet blocks for Ellis when she was baby, and an infant-sized table and chair which sat in the corner of the kitchen until she was big enough to sit at the kitchen table. Later he had made a bookcase for her bedroom, three tiers, that stepped down from a small top shelf where she kept the cow and moon night-light. The bottom shelf still held her collection of Little Golden Books. *The Pokey Little Puppy. The Little Red Hen. The Saggy Baggy Elephant. The Three Little Kittens.* She had wanted the entire set but her father stopped buying them after she turned seven and could read chapter books. You don't need those baby books any more, he had told her.

He had also made a set of chopping boards and a spice rack for Mrs Wood. She had always complained that there was never enough storage or bench space, that the kitchen with its preposterous Early Kooka stove and chipped enamel sink was impossible to cook in. She had got Edgar to agree to replace the old pine table and red-painted chairs with a modern laminex one, with four vinyl and chrome chairs that could be properly wiped clean. Wearing an apron over her plain neat clothes and with her hair always smoothed in its French roll, she would clear this table off every afternoon, putting the bowl of waxed fruit and the cut-glass condiments holder on the dining room dresser. Ellis could then sit at one end and do her homework while at the other Mrs Wood would roll diced meat in seasoned flour or peel vegetables or cut out rounds of puff pastry with a tin cutter, talking through the various steps of the dishes she was cooking.

She taught Ellis how to add a few pinches of curry powder – she favoured Clive of India – to the batter for fried flathead, which took care of the fishy smell in the house. She showed her how to slice cold butter through chilled flour very quickly for a good short pasty, adding lemon juice as well as iced water for a better flavour. She introduced Ellis to her secret for easy scones: full cream instead of the tedious rubbing through with butter then adding milk, which is what the recipes always insisted. Most of this knowledge, she told Ellis, she had gleaned from the women's pages of the Sunday newspapers over the years. She often allowed Ellis to sit at the kitchen table on a Monday afternoon and cut out special recipes or household advice, which she placed in an old shoebox in the pantry.

Now Ellis used the spice rack her father had made, replenishing the curry powder and dried herbs and adding some of her own choosing: cinnamon sticks, bay leaves and whole peppercorns. She had saved Vegemite jars to form something like a matching set, though she had seen a proper set of herb and spice jars, with rounded glass lids and gold labels, in the kitchen shop up the road, which she thought she would get one day.

In those few years the shed had shrunk, or seemed to, and become more cobwebby. The wooden door scraped against piles of dirt and leaves that had accumulated, and the bolt now jammed unless you gave it a good shake before sliding it to the right. She took the hoe from its place against the wall next to the rake and the mower, and returned to scrape the dirt over the ashes this way and that, then a thin layer of leaves.

When she flattened them back with the sole of her shoe, there was nothing to be seen. Nothing at all.

*

AFTER THE OPERATION, Ron had not telephoned her as she had forbade him, telling him they were not to meet or talk ever again, outside of church. To maintain appearances, she still went to the youth group, but decided to go less often. By the start of the new year she would stop going at all and no one would think anything of it. The others in the group already understood that she and Ron were not so close and if their relationship had always been an unspoken one, then their break-up – if that's what it was – was similarly a non-topic. Already she sensed that Ron was turning his attentions to another girl in the fellowship group, Ruth, who was still at school and even younger than she.

Today was the first time she felt normal again, in herself. Not her abdomen, not even her body, but the whole of herself, her spirit and her mind. She had slept badly for weeks, had not been able to concentrate at tech in the evenings. She did not neglect her father or the house, though she did a lot less housework. She caught herself sitting at the kitchen table or on the back step after getting in the washing, doing nothing for long stretches of time. Her father noticed her fatigue, her tendency to eat and talk less at the dinner table. One evening, he put his knife and fork down and said, 'Are you all right, love? Is something wrong?'

'No, nothing. I'm fine. It's just that tech is hard work at the moment.' She cut off a sliver of her meat and pushed it around the gravy.

He looked around the room. 'This old place is hard work too, I suppose.'

She shrugged. 'I don't mind.' Though she did, a bit. It would be better if the place weren't so old-fashioned, if they could have new wall-to-wall carpet and a modern bathroom.

'Maybe it's not such a good idea that you get a job after all. It's not like you need the money.'

'But I want to work.' She put her cutlery down and pushed her plate away. It would perk her up, staying independent, not that she could explain that to him. She was already looking seriously for something full time, and if there was nothing on the horizon right now, she was sure that as soon as businesses reopened after the January break she would find something suitable.

This morning she had risen and gone about her morning tasks feeling as if a heavy cloud had lifted from around her. After her father had read the paper she had opened the Positions Vacant section and circled three ads with a red pencil from the kitchen drawer. Two of the positions were in neighbouring suburbs and one would be perfect to fill in time after college finished. It was in a pharmacy up on the main road, which was expanding to include a large cosmetics counter. She placed the paper to one side of the kitchen table and set about preparing her father's lunch for him to take to work. Two corned beef sandwiches with mustard pickles, an apple and a slice of fruitcake. She had tried salad sandwiches, which he refused to eat. Then substituted the pickles with French mustard from the delicatessen, which he also disliked. She had given him cold roast chicken with a mayonnaise dressing, which she made herself. Tried grated cheese, corn, gherkin relish and shredded lettuce. Every time he thanked her politely enough but asked for corned beef, so she had given up. He even preferred it if she bought it already sliced from the delicatessen, rather than preparing her own cut, which she boiled with peppercorns and herbs, a half-cup of malt vinegar in the water.

She was sorting the laundry when she heard the postman's whistle. Next door's dog darted out from its snoozing place under the hydrangeas and yapped, as it did every weekday the post arrived. In the letterbox was a bill in a window envelope, a copy of *National Geographic* and a bulky envelope, addressed to her, no return address. Intrigued, she opened it up on her way back through the front door and before she got halfway down the hall put her hand to her mouth.

When she saw the photographic paper she was, for one weird split-second, expecting they would be photos of that night. That Ron had perhaps rigged up a secret camera that somehow operated in the dark. Or even worse, pictures of her dead aborted baby. As if either were remotely possible, she realised in the next second when the images, after she turned the six-by-fours around, took shape and she saw exactly what they were.

Ron was completely naked, lying on a bed. He was not looking at the camera, but down at himself, and indeed he looked sad, to be contemplating his own body. She pushed them back into the envelope, her heart beating as though she had performed a criminal act, then took them out again, disbelieving her own eyes. As she did, a piece of folded exercise book paper fell to the floor. Feeling sick, she picked it up. *Thought you would like*, was handwritten, with no preamble, *these photos of your 'boyfriend'. See what he gets up to when you're not around. Notice how he can get an erection for the camera?* It was signed Philip, the name underscored with a thick Z-shaped line that she recognised as distinctly his. In four of the images Ron's penis was in various stages of erection, in the others he was not yet aroused. She had never so much as seen the word erection before, never used it. The word seemed as much an affront as the pictures themselves, and even more offensive was their purpose. And she had never seen Ron's penis before, nor any other. The few nights she and Ron had fumbled their way towards her unexpected pregnancy she had not looked.

By now she knew enough about Philip and his relationship with Ron to understand that it was possible that he was simply trying to intimidate her or bully her. Or just disgust her. Or perhaps, despite the fact that she and Ron had broken up, Philip was still trying to prove he exerted some strange control over Ron. The reason she told Ron months before that she would have nothing more to do with him was not the terrible secret of being pregnant and the trauma of having to terminate it, but because of what Ron had explained to her about himself and Philip.

'Why did you want to be with me then?' she had asked that final night when they had sat in Ron's car, and he had replied that he was trying to prove he was normal. And he thought that he was now ready to get away from Philip's control.

Still, looking at the images one last sickening time before pushing them back into the envelope forever, she wondered why they had been sent to her, now, and when they had been taken. If Philip had taken them while she and Ron were together she did not want to know. She had asked Ron, the last night they spoke, why they had left their previous church and come to St John's.

'The minister there found us out,' Ron had confessed, looking down at the floor of the car. 'And he insisted we stop being friends and go separately to him every week for counselling. Otherwise we had to leave the parish. We tried it for a few months but failed.'

'Who failed?' Ellis had said. 'Was it you or Philip who gave up on trying to be normal?'

He had looked up at her and pushed his hair off his forehead in the gesture she no longer found endearing, then looked away and sighed.

'He did. I felt sorry for him. I couldn't abandon him. He lost his father when he was just a kid and he needed a friend.'

Ellis was too shocked to respond to this. Did he not even remember that her mother had never figured in her life? She looked out the window while Ron prattled on about her not needing to worry, as Philip would be going away soon for his country service, and it would be a long way away, perhaps Griffith or even Broken Hill, and they could get on with their life. By that stage Ellis had made up her mind. She was already reaching for the door handle.

*

AT FIRST SHE SHOVED the photographs under her mattress and sat on top of the bed. Then she got off and stuck them at the bottom of her wardrobe under a shoebox. Then after sitting back on the bed and contemplating everything, her chest heaving, she went to the bathroom and washed and dried her face. Her father would not be back from work until after five. She took the envelope with the photographs and letter – she was not sure now which offended her more – straight out the back and down under the plane trees, taking a box of matches from the top of the stove.

The worst thing, she realised, the greatest betrayal of all, was that Ron would have developed and printed them in the laboratory where he worked. As she set light to them and watched them curl into grey flakes and as she stamped and raked to remove all traces, she had the strange sensation that she was suffocating, perhaps in the earth below the place where she stood right now, and would have to fight very hard to stay alive. She gulped in heaving breaths before she steadied herself and began to feel like she was breathing normally again.

When she was satisfied there was no hint that there had been a fire she returned to the house, went to the kitchen and hauled the potato and onion bin out from under the bench. Grabbing three potatoes and one onion, she tossed them into the sink for peeling then noticed how grubby the bin was. She emptied all the vegetables out, took it outside and hosed it and left it to dry on the lawn while she returned to sweep under the bench with the dustpan and broom. She filled the kettle to boil and while she was waiting pulled everything out, the pedestal garbage bin, the five-tiered saucepan stand, the box where she kept old newspapers and empty jars. Upturning the chairs onto the table she swept the kitchen twice, not brushing the dirt out the back door onto the verandah like she usually did but carefully collecting it in the dustpan. When she went to put it in the bin she realised how grubby that had become too, so she emptied it into the big rubbish bin at the side of the house, took it back to the laundry where she scrubbed it with pine disinfectant then left it on the lawn to dry next to the vegetable bin.

She was exhausted, yet curiously energised. She worked with a steely focus that she did not remember experiencing before, as if her life from now on depended on how well she polished the lino floor or how smooth her cream sauce would be later that evening. She fetched the mop and poured boiling water from the kettle into the bucket, adding a capful of eucalyptus oil to the floor cleaner like Mrs Wood had always done, and mopped the floor so vigorously she felt the sweat blooming in her armpits. Taking down the methylated spirits and a small scrubbing brush she cleaned around the kitchen taps and the top of the stove, then wiped the stove dry before putting the kettle on again. After she put the chairs back she took a clean cloth and wiped the kitchen table with metho, then again with fresh boiling water until the steam rose from the laminex in little clouds. The moisture evaporated by time she smoothed a fresh seersucker cloth over the top and replaced the condiments in the centre. She went through the house and took every cloth and towel, every placemat and runner she could find and went to the laundry to put them on to wash, then returned to the front room with a yellow duster and bottle of polish, and commenced cleaning the window frames, the sideboard, the dining table, every wooden surface she could. In the bathroom she tackled the green stain under the bath taps that usually eluded her most vigorous scrubbing, and took to the taps at the basin with the metho and the nail brush until her eyes watered with the fumes. Back in the kitchen, she was just lining the clean, dry bin with newspaper when her father appeared at the screen door, loosening his tie.

'Sorry, Dad.' Ellis wiped the back of her hand across her forehead. 'I've got carried away with the cleaning. Dinner will be a bit late tonight.'

14

⁋ WHEN THE FLAT WAS CLEARED OF JANE'S
clothes and all the items Dove was sending to charity, when
it was clean and waiting, with minimal furniture to retain
some effect of a home, a sturdy pot plant on the coffee table
and the fridge door propped open almost expectantly, she still
delayed contacting an agent. She had inherited it without any
complications, and she had prepared it to sell and had no use for
it, but she could not pass it on.

She still considered moving in. Her own place in Camperdown
was beginning to feel oppressive. She had little aptitude for
household improvements and none for home making. Her place
was utilitarian, serving a need to be close to the city and work
and, until recently, her mother. She had lived there for the past
three years. It was a half-house, the smaller, poorer section of a

Federation bungalow whose lawns had once sprawled into dense gardens that hugged the walls. The block next to it was originally an orchard for the main house. Her own little front garden bore traces of sandstone borders which her neighbours in the larger part of the house told her was originally a rose garden. Sunlight on the whole building was mostly stolen by the huge native fig trees in the street: heritage orders prevented them from being trimmed. When she had moved in she had felt like a temporary tenant, a feeling that remained. The fruit bats seemed to have more claim to the place than she. They colonised the figs in the street, dropping fruits and excrement, shrieking and flapping at inconvenient times, such as when she was trying to watch the evening news.

Most of the backyard was carpeted with wandering jew, and morning glory covered the fences and twisted around the trees. In the moist summers the place hummed with mosquito life. In the damp winters it was a sodden zone where the climbing weeds lay dormant for a few months, exposing flat rocks that represented a long-distant effort at landscaping. Even if it hadn't rained for weeks the garden was always humid. The smell of wet earth, a rotting potato-in-the-cellar smell, was inescapable.

It seemed to Dove that for the entire time she had lived in Camperdown it had never stopped being wet. Mould appeared on everything – shoes and bags in her wardrobe, the bathroom ceiling, overcoats in the hall cupboard – and she learned to keep a spray bottle of bleach handy in the shower. Outside, the house was just as bad. The front porch flooded in heavy rain, seeping quickly under the front door. She kept a mop there permanently. She had heard of mould spores infiltrating people's lungs and making them ill with chronic coughs and congestion. She had never suffered from chest complaints, but she knew that diseases like asthma could be exacerbated by spores. What impeded her breathing, especially in bed at night, was not the damp.

*

SHE TOOK HER NOTEBOOK and coffee out to the back porch where it was actually sunny this day. Since the dream of Emily on the moors – which was too powerful and lasting for a dream but what else could she call it? – the story had stalled. Without being able to see or imagine what came next, let alone how it fitted in, she would sort out some details about Ellis and sketch out some scenes.

The house in Ashfield she had imagined for Ellis and Edgar was a version of the place she lived in now. And yet it was vastly different in many respects. It was a family home for a start, and while her house might also once have been a large family home, for a long time it had not been anything more than a place for students and single people like herself, more recently inner city working couples. It had been divided back in the 1960s and the scullery and second toilet converted into Dove's kitchen and bathroom. Her front door was the original side or tradesman's entrance. The people next door were lawyers, and those before were student tenants of an elderly Greek couple who sold their side of the house just before Dove moved in. The lawyers had told Dove they were happy here and planned to renovate before starting a family. In the space of less than a decade the inner city suburb had become a desirable place for a young family, with babies fitting into the blossoming hipster lifestyle. She saw these new mothers and fathers everywhere, with three-wheeled prams parked outside tiny cafés, the parents bearded and tattooed and clearly uninterested in departing to the roomier outer suburbs, as was the case back when she was in her early twenties.

Ellis's family home was much larger. Dove saw it standing on its block, not a quarter acre but nevertheless large. She had seen all this clearly right from the start when the story had first come to her, but she made notes anyway: red brick, classic Federation in style right down to the rising sun emblem above the doorway and the rooftop finials. A green wire gate, in need of repainting. The path leading up to the front door, the path where Charlie took his first baby steps, was tessellated, in black, cream and terracotta tiles. Both front and back doors had wire screen doors with timber frames, old-fashioned doors in which Edgar would replace the wire mesh now and then. He had not done this for a while and Dove could see a large gaping tear in the back door that suggested he was too old and frail to bother with this any more. Or perhaps he was no longer there and the house was empty.

When had he stopped doing these sorts of jobs around the house? When had he stopped mowing the lawns with his cherished rotary mower, raking the clippings into neat piles which he then loaded into the wheelbarrow and piled in a heap right at the back fence under the plane trees? When had he organised a local mowing service to come and take care of the front lawn and the large backyard instead? The yard was mainly grass, from the back step all the way down to the shed, which he now rarely entered. When, for that matter, had Ellis's father died?

She did some calculations in her notebook. Edgar might be alive but he would be very old. Ellis herself was now about sixty-five, give or take. She wouldn't still be living there, surely. But she had redecorated some of the rooms, not long before she married Vince. When she returned to live with her father after leaving Vince she must have fixed up the larger spare bedroom, for herself and Charlie, who would have only been one. Meeting and marrying Vince: that was another hole in the narrative she'd have to think about. Halfway through writing this down Dove gave up and shut the notebook. These were imaginary people. None of them was alive, no matter their age.

Despite the sun she could feel the damp seeping from the wooden garden chair through her jeans. Her mother's place had always been dry and airy. Up on the second floor, its windows never shut except in the heaviest rain, it was always light. Yet with the palms so close by, and the lorikeets fussing around every evening, it was like being in the midst of a garden.

Viv emerged from the shade down the back. He tiptoed his way to the step then turned and sat with his back to Dove, his tail whipping from side to side. Her phone beeped. She checked the message: Martin, saying it was quiet in Passageway, to come up for a drink. She thought for moment then texted him back: *No tks. Going to agent about Mum's flat.* But she took her things inside and put on the CD of Turkish music he'd given her, observing from the corner of her eye how Viv sat at a distance and pretended not to care but in fact listened attentively with his neat head to one side, ears twitching. Her mother was right: she had always said that if cats could play a musical instrument it would be the violin. Seated, his head erect, Viv's shape even resembled one. When the gypsy strings kicked in she almost heard his purring and heartbeat joining in the rhythm.

There was no way she could give up this place and move into her mother's flat. The cat had settled right in to the point where she could not imagine how he had lived in a flat all those years, balcony or not. Each morning after breakfast he wailed at the back door then paraded around the garden with his tail like a flagpole, and Dove had stopped worrying when he disappeared for hours. She had installed a cat door. When she arrived home she would hear its flap rattle as Viv raced through, only to stop when he saw her and sit inscrutably on the mat until hunger overcame his feigned indifference. If she called him up from the garden he would appear from behind a bush or jump off the makeshift table down the back, then sidle along the edges of the yard, pausing to sniff leaves and paw at imaginary insects, pretending to ignore her but finally bolting up the steps unable to contain himself, on the chance that food was involved – food which he would then affect to disdain, until she had turned her back on him. The mechanical growling that had accompanied everything he did had now almost vanished, and she no longer woke in the middle of the night to find him anxiously kneading her chest or stomach with his front paws. He was without her mother's music – although she did her best – but in every other way the cat's life was transformed. She watched him almost trembling with pleasure in the music. She couldn't confine him again.

15

––––––

❦ THE FIRST TIME SHE MET VINCE SHE recognised that, like her, he was quiet and dependable. He rarely smiled but his demeanour was not to be mistaken for that of someone sour or gloomy. She met him on her first day at Rose's Automotives, on his way back to the workshop after lunch, when he stepped inside the office.

'I'm Vince,' he said. 'Welcome aboard.'

'Thank you.' So far that first day none of the other men had spoken with her. Mr Rose himself was busy and Shirley, though she was pleasant enough, was preoccupied with her retirement plans, interrupting herself numerous times to make telephone calls to removalists and agents – 'I don't have a home phone, and Mr Rose doesn't mind' – instead of explaining to Ellis how the office was run. And when she did explain, she told Ellis things she didn't need to know, like how to set out an account or why they needed to deduct tax from the weekly pay. She hadn't listened when Ellis had told her she'd recently completed a book-keeping certificate and had been doing that anyway for the past two years at the pharmacy, where she'd worked part time. All she needed to know were things like where Shirley kept the carbon paper and who their regular suppliers were. She was seated at her desk holding up a stack of grease-spotted invoice books and wondering where to store them when Vince appeared.

'We're a bit rough, but the men are a decent bunch,' he added, as if he thought that was her biggest concern. Out in the yard behind the workshop she could hear them laughing and joking as they prepared to get back to work. She had seen him half an hour earlier go out for lunch, unlike the other men, taking his sandwich from the order basket that the newest apprentice had brought back from the corner shop.

Should she step out from behind the desk and shake his hand, or just sit there smiling? What was the correct way to deal with men at work? There was a hierarchy, she knew, and most of the men wouldn't even dream of entering the office, but stayed just outside the doorway in their grimy shoes, rubbing their hands with a rag. She noticed how clean his hands were, that he carried a folded newspaper and when he smiled his face transformed. Before she could speak Shirley bustled back into the office.

'Vince, you've met our new girl, Ellis? Now don't go holding her up, not on her first day.'

Ellis and Vince smiled at each other over Shirley's broad cheerful back. Orange and white polka dots were not what she would wear at that age, Ellis thought.

Rose's Automotives had only ever employed one part-time woman in the office but the older Mr Rose told Ellis when she applied for the job that the business was expanding, and that the role might be full time soon.

Shirley was a war widow, she explained that first morning, and her three grandchildren were quickly growing up and why would she keep working? She was moving into a smaller place that the people at Legacy had found her, and the first thing she was doing after she settled in was going on a long P&O cruise with her closest friend. Of course it would take her several months just to clean out the old home in Haberfield, which she and Clem had built when they were first married.

By the end of her first week Ellis had spoken once or twice more with Vince, each time noting he was somehow different. The other men were noisier, though quiet, almost deferential when they encountered her, but Vince seemed not to change the way he spoke around her: he had the same measured, slow manner, and she never heard him yelling out bloodys and shits like the other men did when they were under a car and thought no one could hear, especially Mr Rose, who hated swearing. Vince always went out for lunch and always seemed to have something to read, even if it was only the *Daily Telegraph*.

On the Friday, Shirley's last day, Ellis brought in a large plate of cakes, to hold a farewell afternoon tea. She thought that lamingtons and her home-made miniature sausage rolls would be easy for the men to eat: she couldn't see butterfly cupcakes or meringues in their large grease-stained hands.

'You made these yourself?' Shirley said, handing around the lamingtons to the three apprentices. Ellis nodded. 'You'll make someone a fine wife one day, I reckon.' Ellis turned away to the crate of soft drinks that Mr Rose had supplied as a treat, pulling out a bottle of Coca-Cola. Vince reached in and took it from her, holding the bottle opener.

'Here, let me.' He opened it and then one for himself, turning around to listen as Mr Rose stood on the hoist to say a few words of farewell. He clinked his bottle against hers. 'Cheers,' he said, and winked.

*

OVER THE NEXT FEW WEEKS, on her afternoons off and the weekends, she worked on modernising the front room, having realised they hardly ever sat there any more, it was so gloomy and uncongenial. She removed the prints of John Constable landscapes in their pigs' ear gilt frames, and made slip covers for the Jacobean lounge suite that had been there all her life. She couldn't disguise the dark carved frame but made new beige covers for the tapestry seats, which she broke up with scatter cushions in purple, orange and red. She threw out the dried flower arrangements and put away the heavy ornaments that were neither useful nor pleasing to look at – squat vases that barely held a stem, a series of shepherdess figurines that were impossible to keep clean, silver-plate fruit bowls that they had never used but which she recalled Mrs Wood polishing with Silvo, month after month – items that had sat there since her father was a boy and which he kept from indifference or reverence for previous generations who had long departed the world. Along the mantelpiece, which she painted cream, she placed thick short candles, orange and scented. The old dark brown carpet square that had also been there forever was banished to the back sunroom and the floor was now polished boards.

She kept her father out of the room until it was finished, then surprised him.

'Ta da!' She opened the door the morning it was all done, and ushered him in.

Edgar blinked, exaggerating the light.

'What do you think?'

'Well . . . it's a bit bare isn't it?' He went over to the mantelpiece, picked a candle up and sniffed it, replacing it carefully.

'You never use it anyway.' She could tell he was impressed with her efforts, even if it wasn't to his taste. He preferred the smaller sitting room across the hall where he told her that her grandparents had kept a card table covered in a green cloth and where they had entertained weekly, with sherry in decanters and ham sandwiches and pipe tobacco, the scent of which Ellis swore she could still catch every time she went in there.

The card table was long packed away but the old wireless stood in a corner with a pot plant on the top. Her father had set up the television and his easy chair, one that tilted backwards and supported the legs with side levers, which he had bought anticipating his retirement.

In the refurbished living room, Ellis sat and read and played records on her portable player, sometimes doing her craftwork or just painting her nails. When Vince called on her one Sunday afternoon they sat there listening to music and chatting until her father arrived home from a game of bowls.

He called out his usual 'Hi de hi!', rapping at the doorway over the sound of the Beatles singing 'We Can Work It Out'. She turned the record player off.

'Hi Dad. This is Vince.'

Vince had arrived with a bunch of carnations for Ellis which she'd placed on the coffee table. He now produced a bottle of tawny port for Edgar.

'I'll make us all some coffee.' Ellis went to the kitchen.

Her father and Vince talked about decimal currency and Jørn Utzon's sacking and when she returned with the tray they had moved on to Holden's installation of seat belts and the plans to introduce drink driving as an offence. Vince responded to Edgar's slightly formal questions with respectful gravity, with the same calm ease as when he was discussing spark plugs or gaskets at work. He seemed to be a man entirely sure of himself, which Ellis found intriguing. It was not something she recognised in herself.

It was a bit ridiculous in this day and age, and rather staged, for them to be sitting awkwardly in the front room with coffee in the percolator going cold and Vince unwilling to seem rude and take the last piece of lemon slice, but Ellis had known her father would appreciate this sort of introduction. It would be better than having Vince casually say hello after bringing her home from a date. And it was nothing like her previous relationship with Ron. She briefly closed her eyes then opened them again, picking up the cake plate.

'Vince, please eat this. I'll only have to throw it away.'

'What about this war, then?' Edgar was saying. It sounded like a test, but she knew it was just his manner.

'I don't really approve. Hard to understand it all, isn't it?'

'What if you're called up?'

'Of course I'd go. You have to do your duty.'

'Vince's brother has already gone,' Ellis said. Gary was now in Phuoc Tuy Province where most of the Australians were based. It would look bad if his brother were to object.

Predictably, thought Ellis, the talk moved on to politics.

'Mr Holt is doing an okay job so far, don't you think?' This time Vince got in first, testing the water.

'Considering Menzies is a hard act to follow.'

Vince nodded, not quite confident enough to commit himself.

'Time will tell,' her father added.

She was gratified to hear that Vince understood there were certain responses. But after a few more minutes of polite evasive talk she interrupted.

'Vince, it's okay. Dad always votes Labor even though he's in banking.'

He father sat back with a small smile. When Vince left, he shook his hand, clasping it with the other. 'Call me Edgar,' he said.

*

AFTER THAT IT ALL UNFOLDED as if it were meant to be. It was not a white wedding, nor an elaborate one. Instead Ellis made herself a duck egg blue slub silk dress with close-fitting chiffon sleeves and long buttoned cuffs, with matching satin ribbon under the bustline. The skirt came to the knees. Although she had thought about a short one like Sharon Tate had worn recently, she realised this would offend Vince's mother, possibly also her own father, even though he was more accepting of her modern dress sense. Vince's mother, on the other hand, was a strict Presbyterian and coming to the wedding at St John's, small as it was, was enough of a compromise on her behalf. She sat with her second husband wearing her best frock, a capacious one patterned in pink cabbage roses, which had clearly been worn many times before, judging by the yellowed underarms. She wore brown lace-up shoes and carried a faux crocodile handbag, and fanned herself during the service with a large man's handkerchief. Her hair had been permed tightly.

Mr Curry wore a dark brown suit with a handkerchief card in the top pocket. He took Ellis's hand after the service and told her to call him Harry. 'Harry Curry,' he joked mildly. 'Not a name people forget in a hurry. Get it?'

There were no bridesmaids, and no best man as Vince's closest friend was away, and Gary was not due for leave any time soon. Even if they had planned the wedding around him there was no guarantee that he would come, as according to Vince he was unreliable. On his last leave, he'd gone off up the north coast with mates, not even staying one night with his family after arriving back in Sydney.

As they stood at the altar Ellis made her vows in a clear voice. She did love him, in a way. And she did honour him and believed obeying him would be entirely possible. But as Vince slid the ring onto her finger she also believed she could feel Mrs Curry's small brown eyes from the second row, boring through her back past the blue slub silk and seeing all the way into her womb. Of course, she could just have been suspicious that they'd decided to get married so early, not six months after they first met, and that the wedding was so small. But Ellis couldn't shake off the uneasy feeling that Vince's mother had also seen all the way through her, and seen what she herself knew to be there. Damage and violation, and more: an emptiness that might never be filled.

As she and Vince walked down the aisle she ducked her head, feeling like a physical blow once more the absence of her own mother, who should have been sitting there in the first row, elegant legs crossed at the ankles, wearing a skirt suit in pale pink or apricot. Perhaps a tiny pillbox hat in the same fabric, with a wisp of veil, the colour contrasting beautifully with her dark wavy hair, which Ellis believed she had inherited.

She would not cry, she could not cry, but she felt like it, especially when they got past the porch to see Mrs Wood waiting outside.

'You came after all,' Ellis said, when she could control her voice.

Mrs Wood had been invited – Ellis had hand-delivered the invitation – but they had not heard a word.

Mrs Wood said nothing until after she embraced Ellis, then whispered in her ear. 'I didn't want to. But I realised I had to.' She removed her sunglasses briefly, adjusted her hat, then held out a gloved hand to Vince. 'And this must be the lucky man.'

They went for lunch afterwards, just a dozen of them, at the local workers' club in Ashfield, where Mr Rose talked about feeling like a father towards Vince, but how Vince's father George had been a fine man who would have been proud today, while Mrs Curry clutched her handkerchief and Harry looked into his lap. Billy, the eldest of the Rose boys, who had done engineering at university, proposed the toast. Vince's friend Mack made a speech with all the right jokes, and his wife Betty took her aside in the ladies' before the cake was cut and asked her in a quiet voice if there was anything she needed to know, Ellis not having had a mother. They had only just met, she said, but Ellis was welcome to ask her anything and Betty would explain, having been married for years by now. 'Thank you, Betty,' she said. 'But I'll be right.'

Ellis had made the cake, a single tier of simple design decorated with real baby roses, which stood on a table of its own. Aside from that there was no suggestion this was a wedding celebration. If they had had a private party, they could not have served alcohol with Mrs Curry there, and if they'd gone to a proper reception house Ellis would have found the formality and the lack of guests unbearable. Her father had suggested the club, which had a private room and a balcony, and where the drinkers could nip out and buy themselves a beer at the bar if they liked. Harry Curry barely said a word and Mrs Curry, who never invited Ellis to call her Muriel or Mum, stared around her, when she was not staring at Ellis's stomach. They left as soon as the speeches were over, before the cake was handed around.

The new couple spent the night at the Great Southern Hotel, so they could catch the early train to the south coast the next morning. While Vince was cleaning his teeth in the bathroom down the hall Ellis sat on the bed and wondered what to say to him.

'Happy?' he said, coming back to the room.

'Yes. Of course I am.'

He gathered her close and they lay there, he in his boxer shorts and white singlet, she in her nightie. He kissed her on the brow first, then her nose, then her lips.

She was happy. Or at least content. She would owe him so much.

In the end she said nothing and while he kissed her throat, leaned over to turn out the bedside light before helping him slip her nightie off. If he thought anything was amiss then perhaps he put it down to his own inexperience.

Afterwards, Ellis lay awake for a long time, watching the moon and the streetlights slanting through the room, listening to the whistles and sirens and occasional call from the footpath below.

16

⁌ THE NEXT PART OF THE STORY, SHE already knew, involved Charlie, since the pregnancy occurred soon after Ellis and Vince married. But Dove had run out of ideas. When the baby was born, she had a fair idea, but exactly where, and how, resisted her imagination. Doubtless because she had no experience in this respect, she could not bring herself to visualise a pregnancy and the birth of a baby. She knew that this was nonsense, if she were to call herself a writer of fiction, and that she needed to do something about this, even if it simply meant googling the subject. After that, she should hang around the post-natal ward of the nearby hospital. She knew that when the story stalled like this the best thing was always to get moving. Aside from this, the more reasons to get her out of the house the better, since she'd become so

ridiculously isolated. Yet she found herself curiously unwilling
to get out and about.

Nevertheless she made the effort one morning and walked
through the back streets from her home and across Missenden
Road to the main part of the hospital. She passed a cluster of
white-gowned patients chatting furtively under a huge moody
fig. They looked to Dove like they were trading medications.
Three ibis flapped around on the overfull rubbish bin, pulling
at a tomato sauce-stained white wrapper before screeching and
flying up to perch in the fig tree. Outside the emergency ward
two women in tracksuits were smoking over a child who seemed
far too old to be in a stroller. One of the women pushed the
stroller back and forth in time with rapid desperate draws on
her cigarette. Dove waited for an ambulance to enter and park,
and then another that followed straight away as if there were
some major accident nearby. Partly from interest, she stopped
and sat on the low brick fence outside the McCafé and watched
as each ambulance reverse parked and opened their doors to
disgorge their contents. On a high gurney all that was visible was
the cloud of white hair of a patient covered in a blanket. From
another emerged a young man, staggering and resisting the
ambo who followed him, holding up a plastic saline pack that
led to his bandaged arm. Why wasn't he strapped to a gurney,
she wondered. The man's good arm waved about aggressively
causing the ambo to duck while she was trying to keep the saline
line intact. Within minutes the ambulance bay was crowded
with blue uniforms.

She ordered a coffee, waiting in the queue for a ridiculous length of time given there was only one other customer, while the staff behind the counter bickered or ignored each other. After the first sip she wondered why she had even thought a McCafé flat white would satisfy her. No, she didn't need to wonder: for some reason she was delaying her task. She threw the coffee away and walked back into the hospital and took the lift to the post-natal ward. Staring through the double glass doors that led to the main ward, she could see several women wheeling babies in clear plastic cots down the hall. She pushed through the doors and followed them down the hall herself. Rooms to her right and left held single beds, about half of them occupied. Only a few had curtains around the beds, and most of them had the plastic cot parked next to them. At a bend there was a nurses' station, with two staff with their backs to her peering at computer monitors. Farther along was a sitting room where a woman and her baby were surrounded by family. Past the bend were more rooms, most with their doors ajar. She peeked into one to find the patient asleep, her baby beside her.

At the end of the ward was a lounge room where several women were feeding their babies and chatting. Smiling, as if she belonged here, was maybe just lost on her way to visit a sister or friend, Dove turned and walked back. Strangely there was hardly any noise. If she had imagined anything before she arrived, it would have been the swollen collective sound of babies crying at the top of their lungs. Instead, a few faint kittenish wails broke the silence now and then. She paused to let a midwife bustle past with an armload of folders. Another approached glued to a phone and hauling a blood pressure monitor along with her. She smiled again and paused at a room that held two women and babies, all four of them asleep.

There appeared to be few other visitors. As this was a public hospital no one would challenge her. There were signs about strict visiting hours but no evidence of security, and she could probably walk in and out all day before a nurse thought to question her. Perhaps never. In a room back near the entrance to the ward, the bed was empty and the bathroom next to it occupied. Beside the bed in its plastic cot the small white mound looked like it was all parcelled up and ready to post off somewhere. She was mere feet from the baby. The sound of a shower running came from the bathroom.

A weird but urgent thought struck her. She – anyone – could just reach out and take this baby and head off. How long before one of those preoccupied nurses would notice and buzz for security? When the mother awoke or emerged from the shower, how many minutes would a baby thief have to get away with her spoils? It would take all of a minute to walk out of the ward, run down the stairs and out the door. The hospital was close to the university, and there was a connecting path. She could disappear in there within minutes. Or she could be bold and walk straight up the road and hail a taxi, where they were all lined up just past the McCafé. It would be almost no time before she would be speeding off to any destination.

Why was she thinking like this? She had not the remotest desire for a baby, and yet she had to stop herself from creeping forward. Another step or two and she could place her hand on it. Feeling foolish and even guilty, she quickly walked back down the hall and out the doors to the lift. A persistent image stuck in her mind: a baby wrapped up just like that one, like a parcel, being borne along by some woman who was not its mother.

She walked back home the long way, all the way up to King Street, to have a proper coffee with Martin and tell herself there was nothing wrong. When she explained the strange compulsion to him he shrugged and said, 'Must be what it's like, being a fiction writer. Lucky you're not writing about a murder or something.'

Dove spluttered over her coffee. 'God. Don't make it worse for me.'

Back home, writing up her notes actually helped. She realised that back in Ellis's day hospitals were more controlled and authoritarian, and new mothers were especially regimented. Ellis of course would resist much of that. Her independence was by now very clear. Even when they announced they were expecting, it was a casual moment. Ellis had merely dropped in to visit her mother-in-law one afternoon on her way home from work. She travelled to Rose's Automotives with Vince but got the bus home, leaving at lunchtime. Mr Rose had never made her position full time and now she was glad only to be working mornings.

When she told her mother-in-law, she could see her mind rapidly calculating behind her glasses, and she couldn't help feeling a stab of satisfaction that Mrs Curry's suspicions had been unfounded. By the time Charlie was born – a definite eleven months after the wedding – Mrs Curry had softened enough to get out her knitting needles and old pattern books, discreetly tucking them away whenever Vince and Ellis visited.

The birth was at Crown Street Women's Hospital, Dove decided. She still could not get her head around the specifics of the event, and she couldn't even get into Ellis's head to experience it from her point of view, but she knew it went smoothly enough, considering it was her first. Anyway, she was efficient at everything she did, so would be at this. Plus she deserved it, a straightforward birth.

Vince was not allowed in. He walked up and down Crown Street, ducking inside and up the stairs, pacing the waiting room, sharing cigarettes with two other new fathers. Five hours later, just before midnight, the baby arrived. Vince tossed his umpteenth cigarette into the sand box before a nurse appeared for him at the door.

'A lovely healthy boy, Mr Linton.'

He followed her down to the delivery ward where he was draped in a gown and given a mask. Ellis looked pale and her lips were redder than normal, her eyes deeper blue and dark with fatigue. He kissed her, then the damp top of the head of his new son.

'Can we call him Charles?' They'd not seriously discussed names, deciding to wait to find out if it was a girl or a boy, but Vince had mentioned an older brother who had died when he was a baby. Sometimes whenever Muriel was difficult, which had been often when he was young, he thought of how much this had affected her. In an instant, holding the baby that Ellis now held out to him, he knew beyond a doubt: of course it had, of course.

'He doesn't look like a Charles,' Ellis said. 'But he could be a Charlie.'

Vince went to the pay phone on the ground floor to ring Edgar and then the neighbour next door to his mother, as she had never had the phone connected.

The next evening after work, he arrived with a tissue-wrapped parcel from his mother which Ellis opened to reveal a perfect baby's layette: bonnet, booties and jacket, all in the best quality Paton's cream wool, knitted in delicate moss stitch with satin ribbons for fastening.

Ellis was sitting up in a chair, dressed in normal clothes – loose slacks and one of Vince's old pullovers – under her dressing gown.

'Could you fetch him for us?'

'Are they meant to be taken from the nursery?' he said, looking around the ward which held five other new mothers but no babies. He had passed them all in the nursery on his way through, a dozen of them wrapped and quiet in their identical cribs, like a clutch of new eggs, the matron in her white peaked hat keeping guard.

'But my arms are empty, Vince. Look.' She held them up, and indeed her whole body propped in the chair looked shrunken.

'When is he due for feeding?'

'It doesn't matter,' she said. 'Come on, let's take him home.'

17

———

ELLIS, DOVE KNEW, HAD EXPERIENCED nightmares on a regular basis. One of these involved her in an operating theatre on a hospital gurney, having been to all intents placed under an anaesthetic. Except she was fully conscious. Her limbs were trapped beside her, her entire body remained inert and not even her lips or eyelids were able to move to indicate she was not ill, not suffering, and did not require this operation. It pained Dove to know that there was nothing Ellis, or she, could do to indicate her terror. Each time she experienced it, the nightmare took her a little further into the story, but never to an end where she would wake up while still in the dream, to explain to the waiting doctors and nurses that she was perfectly all right, and that this operation, whatever it was for, was unnecessary. Each time she woke while the dream still had her trapped, mute and helpless, and each time she was in a fever of fear, believing that something was about to go wrong in this operation and that she would die while still anaesthetised, and no one would ever know what happened. After several seconds of gasping and looking about her bedroom in the dark, with her sweaty nightclothes pushed off her, Ellis would calm down and lie back on her pillow, her eyes wide and unblinking. It would be ages before she fell asleep again.

And each time Dove looked on as helpless as ever.

When she first pictured that scene she had no idea why Ellis would have such a nightmare – which then became her nightmare – but now, many months later, she thought she began to understand why. The worst instance of this nightmare was of course real, when Ellis had been at the abortionist's, as a frightened sixteen year old. After that the nightmares waned, but returned when she was pregnant, and again when she was giving birth.

Vince, waiting down the hall, or pacing Crown Street, could have no understanding of the ordeal, not just the physical pain, but the pain she felt deep in her heart when she recalled the girl she was not so many years ago who'd endured that operation. During the birth they had approached her with ether for the pain and she had screamed in terror. Thinking it was the pain of labour they had held her down and tried more firmly to apply the ether, but she had thrashed her head viciously and yelled at them to get away. Later that night, after Charlie had arrived, pink and robust, and innocent of the ordeal that had brought him into the world, and Vince had left, glowing with love, she had fallen into a light doze and dreamed the dream yet again, the one that was more like a waking nightmare. She was desperate to get away from this hospital, with its lights and its smells and its lino that reminded her of that evening a few years before.

But after they went home she continued to dream this hideous dream during all the months she was learning to be Charlie's mother. Sometimes it came with variations. For instance, she was still pregnant with him, and it was as if he were to be harmed by the mysterious operation that was about to take place entirely against her will.

She had again dreamed this the night they returned from the Denmans' anniversary barbecue. She had gone to bed exhausted with the effort of maintaining herself all night when she had known since earlier in the evening, from the moment she and Vince had set out in the car, with Charlie in his basket beside the platter of asparagus rolls on the back seat, that the marriage could not continue. After settling Charlie into his cot and changing into her nightie she left Vince sitting on the back step having a final cigarette and went to bed where she lay in the dark looking at the ceiling.

She should have slapped Les hard on the face, there in Betty's kitchen, rather than being so forgiving. She should have screamed at him or fetched his wife or told Vince, who might have taken him out the front and thumped him one; just done something rather than let him get away with that violation. And on Betty's

147

wedding anniversary, poor Betty Denman who longed more than anything for a child.

Dove watched her turn over and face away from the door. Exhausted from the confrontation with herself, with accepting that being Vince's wife, or anyone's, was not possible for her, she was unable to sleep. When she finally did, hours after Vince came and murmured into her hair, she slipped into the uneasy dozing of the insomniac, where dreams merged into real life. Charlie's cries penetrated one of these dreams, and she panicked at not being able to reach him. That was when the operating theatre nightmare took her one step further, where she looked down on her gowned stomach and realised she was carrying him, about six or seven months. At the same time she could hear him crying. There was no logic, but then there never was, in such a dream.

Again she reached into consciousness and pulled herself as hard as she could into waking, sitting up in bed for a few seconds, momentarily blind and terrified, until her eyes adjusted to the dark and she heard the familiar wails coming from the next room. Charlie only needed picking up and rocking for a few minutes to calm him but she sat down in the wicker chair anyway and settled him on her shoulder where he made contented animal noises as he sucked his fist and drifted back to sleep. She wrapped him firmly into his bunny rug and placed him back in the cot, patting his back while his breathing slowed and deepened.

It took her a few more months before she found the courage to tell Vince. She waited until Charlie was asleep one evening and they sat on the back step overlooking the shared garden where next door's washing was still on the line.

'You are the best of men, and I can't explain it. I'm so sorry. All I know is I can't stay married.'

It was beyond horrible. Vince cried, and she did not. She hugged him around his shaking shoulders, and went into their bedroom to start sorting her things.

But it was another month before she told her father. That was when Charlie was one, the day she was visiting Edgar on the bus, the very first time Dove had encountered her in her own imagination. The day she set Charlie down on the garden path and he took his first steps, and Edgar opened the door to say his familiar 'Hi de hi', only for his face to fall as she scooped Charlie up and said, 'I'm leaving Vince. I might have to come home for a while. If that's all right.'

The nightmare stopped altogether and she began to sleep again. She found a nursery school position for Charlie and then a three-days-a-week job back at the pharmacy in Liverpool Road where she'd worked before.

Edgar and Vince met occasionally, and after these meetings her father would come home and try to talk to her, but she would not be coaxed, would not listen.

'You've left him to work in a *chemist?*' He shook his head.

'It's not that simple,' she said. 'I'm working there so I don't bludge off you.'

And she was marking time at the chemist, that was all. She would find her way and who she was meant to be – she knew that somehow, even though in her head it didn't make any sense either.

*

ONE NIGHT SHE WOKE, having in her sleep heard Charlie crying, who now slept in a cot at the foot of her bed in her old bedroom, though he was nearly three and needed a room of his own. He was not crying, he rarely woke at night now, but she had heard him in the dream, crying so loudly and piteously it was as if he was protesting on her behalf the fate she was about to undergo on that operating table. Or it was as if he was protesting the suffering that he was about to feel himself. Drawing up her knees to her chin she sat there for the remainder of the night, just as she used to when she was a girl, looking at the cow and moon night-light that her father had retrieved from the cupboard after Charlie had come along.

Dove watched her begin to pack. Charlie's clothes and night nappies, his toys. His Bunnykins bowl and mug, the silver spoon and fork set that Mrs Wood had given him when he was christened and without which he refused to eat. His little gumboots, bright blue, and his Peter Pan bag that he took on outings. It would all fit into two suitcases. In a box she would pack the night-light too, and the various toys and books that Charlie was beginning to accumulate. As soon as she could that morning she would ring Vince. He had always said he would look after Charlie, whatever happened. It was far better to do all this now rather than in a year or two when there would be too many other complications, such as kindergarten. And the older Charlie became the worse it would get for him. For all of them.

18

❦ SHE DIDN'T KNOW THE EXACT LOCATION
of the place so she left the bus and walked up to King Street from
City Road. On her right the park sloped down to the duck pond
before ascending to meet the iron rail fence of the university. The
weather was unseasonably hot and only a few ducks could be
seen on the water, which was thick and green as pea soup. A few
students were lying on the grass under the trees, others walking
along the paths, heads down, knitted jackets tied by the arms
around their waist. A couple of students wore academic gowns.
They were from the colleges, she assumed, who were expected
to dress formally for lectures. Farther up, she passed the gates of
the university itself, then the college of St Paul's, overshadowed
by Moreton Bay fig trees. Only then she realised she could have
walked through the university itself, something that occurred

to her as a bold, novel idea. But then she was embarking on something new today, and walking through a place where she had never set foot would seem an appropriate thing to be doing. Next time she could just walk through the grounds. She could follow the map in a street directory, and no one, she expected, would take any notice of her, let alone challenge her presence.

The typesetting shop was not far along King Street, she discovered, and just off the main road in a side street that was barely more than a laneway. It had a bland concrete front with three steps leading into a recessed door. There were weeds growing through the cracks in the footpath beside the steps, and shards of brown bottle glass that had been kicked to one side.

As soon as Ellis entered she registered a thrill inside her that she could not quite understand. She took off her sunglasses. The place seemed vast and filthy, dark in the corners, yet illuminated by great skylights which on a second glance were only transparent panels of fibreglass set into the corrugated iron roof. A regular *thuck-thuck* noise was coming from one of the machines. Before her was a long desk, just above waist height, behind that smaller desks with a few people seated. The man nearest to her was wearing a green visor and holding up a long roll of printed material which he was scrutinising through gold-rimmed glasses. When he saw her enter he rose and came over to the larger desk, which she could now see was covered in a variety of printed matter, some individual documents, others in small neat stacks. Pamphlets, magazines, newsletters and posters.

'Can I help you?'

'I've come about a job.'

He took off his glasses, revealing a younger face. He had deep-set grey eyes, and curly hair longer than most young men's.

'A job? That's Clive you want, probably.' He turned around and scanned the room. 'Clive,' he called out. A man in dark blue overalls appeared from behind a stack of cardboard boxes. 'There's a lady here wants a job.'

'What job?' Clive pulled a handkerchief out of his pocket and wiped his face, smoothing his moustache on either side as he walked over to Ellis. Underneath his overalls he wore a business shirt and a brown and fawn striped tie, the knot tied very tightly.

Ellis realised she had not planned this far. She tucked her sunglasses into her handbag and pulled her jacket a little tighter over her shoulders.

'Well, it's about a job I would like to have. To do. Making type.'

The men exchanged a brief glance before the first man raised his eyebrows – not unkindly – and returned to his desk.

'We don't do that,' Clive said.

'But I thought you made type.'

'Well yes, we do. But it's dirty work.' He nodded towards the rear of the premises where Ellis could see several more men in overalls standing or sitting at large machines. She had already done some research in the library and determined that a business such as this would almost certainly be using designs made by Monotype. But typesetters and printers also made their own designs. Perhaps she had made a mistake. Perhaps she had misjudged this sort of business. She had hoped that its proximity to the university would mean it was something one might call creative. Progressive. She had read an article about the flourishing of the type design business. She had consulted all the books on the subject she could find, and then pored over a book on calligraphy, just for the heck of it.

She swallowed her disappointment. 'I was hoping to get some work designing types,' she said. She pulled a manila folder out of her handbag and placed it on the counter between them.

Clive shook his head. 'We don't do that here, love. One of the boys might do something artistic now and then, like Tom over there.'

At the sound of his name the man she first spoke to raised his head and stared at her, then dropped his gaze to his desk again. Unlike the other men he wore brown corduroy trousers, a loose shirt and a vest, unbuttoned. Perhaps he was an art student.

'But it takes time,' Clive said. 'A lot of work involved. We can't afford that. Besides . . .' He paused, appraising Ellis.

'Yes?'

'Women don't make type.'

A few yards away a woman was seated at a desk in front of a typewriter. Behind her silver cat's-eye glasses it was not clear if she was listening in to the conversation or not. On the desk beside her typewriter was a green cut-glass vase containing pink carnations, on the other side a three-tiered wooden out-tray. She watched the woman wind up the sheet in the machine, a nervous attenuated clicking as she did so, then apply a flat round eraser, which was attached by string to the typewriter, to a spot in the middle of the page. She blew on the page then wound the sheet down and continued typing. It was something that she herself had done hundreds of times over.

'They use it though,' she said softly.

Clive chewed at his bottom lip under his moustache. 'Never heard of a woman in the business before,' he finally said.

Ellis looked at the floor. It was time she left this place. Why did she want to make type anyway? It wasn't like there weren't enough of them around. Helvetica. Courier. German Gothic. Baskerville. Century. Copperplate. Some of these she was familiar with from her reading, others she had learned when taking her stenographer and secretarial courses at evening college. But she had always loved the shapes of letters. The calligraphy book she had borrowed from the library contained blank lined pages covered with tracing paper, intended for the owner to practise various styles. She had sat at the kitchen table at night and traced over the letters with a soft lead pencil, considering how she might contrive to keep the book and fill those pages using a nib pen and ink, as was intended. But Miss Neville, the librarian, now knew her far too well for her to get away with such a crime. Ellis had been in the habit of browsing there for an hour or so a few mornings each week. It was located in the basement of the Town Hall in Ashfield and was a dim, quiet place frequented by few people. She had started going when she had realised she needed to get herself and Charlie out of the house on her days off, to let them both breathe – to let herself breathe, the house oppressed her so. Before inspecting the shelves, she read the Positions Vacant in the *Sydney Morning Herald* and made notes of businesses she might contact. Typesetting came after Secretarial and Stenographers, which was how she had got the idea.

As a child she had had a set of alphabet building blocks. Her father had produced them from a cupboard storage box for Charlie. They had raised serif capital letters, like large stamps, painted in different colours. A was red, G was green, B was yellow – she remembered that from when she was a small girl. Touching them for the first time again, she could see an adult hand helping her build a tower, G, H, B, C, K, and she wanting the block for E, the letter for her name, and becoming fretful when she could not find it. Then her own wilful hand swiping the blocks down. There were tears. The adult had no face, was just arms and legs, a tall body bent over. Perhaps it was her father, though somehow she instinctively knew it was not. Possibly a carer. Not her mother. It could not have been her mother.

'I love letters,' she now found herself saying, though why she could not tell. It was not the sort of information she imagined Clive or anyone in the typesetting factory would care to know. The man in the green visor glanced up from his desk again. She should leave before she embarrassed herself further, but then her mouth, working as if it were a completely autonomous thing, uttered more. 'I just love the shapes,' she said, 'the endless possibilities.'

'You a reader?' Clive said.

'Oh yes. I love reading. I love words.'

Under her jacket and ribbed turtleneck top, Ellis began to feel warm with the nonsensical shame of it. She would have liked to take the jacket off, but that would have signified something else – familiarity, or an intention to settle in at this place. She remained hot, hoping her face was not becoming flushed. Reading was something you were meant to like, to respect, not be passionate about. Not admit love for it.

If Clive noticed she was becoming uncomfortable he did not say.

'My wife's a great reader,' he offered. 'She's reading *Love Story* at the moment. Me, I can't finish a book. Prefer my magazines.'

She could have embraced him for his kindness. She cleared her throat. 'I enjoyed that novel,' she said, forcing a restraint into her voice that normally came naturally to her. Besides, she had enjoyed it, not loved it. 'But language is . . .' she said. 'Words are . . .'

'Yes?'

'Words. You can't create a new word. But you can change the way they look. With letters. Typefaces, I mean.'

Ellis was beginning to feel quite troubled with herself. She had come expecting to be able to apply for a job, and here she was indulging in an aesthetic discussion. Clive ran his finger between his collar and neck, easing the tie looser. She noticed now that his shirt was rather grubby, with a bloom of sweat along the collar line. Mr Rose at Vince's garage was like that, wearing a business shirt under his overalls. Vince had always changed into a dark blue T-shirt under his overalls, no matter the weather, dressing in day clothes again before leaving for home each afternoon. She had always soaked Vince's work clothes in the laundry tub after rubbing the greasy stains with hot water and a bar of Sard Wonder Soap. Each evening after he returned home and showered he would scrub his hands with a nail brush then scrape under each fingernail with the blade of his penknife. She wondered if Vince was as fastidious about his work clothes now that she was no longer washing them, or if someone else was taking care of that for him.

'Sorry, love,' Clive was saying. 'But if anything comes up we'll give you call. When Marjorie here goes on holidays' – he jerked his head to the woman at the typewriter – 'maybe you could step in.'

'Oh, I don't want to type. I already do that.'

The look on Clive's face now turned. It spoke a thousand words, a story of disapproval. How women really shouldn't work at all, and how she should be grateful she'd got an offer like this, and such a sympathetic hearing in the first place. Behind his frown Ellis imagined she could see him thinking how presumptuous it was of her to walk in here to ask for work, to expect an opportunity, and how audacious it was for a woman to refuse even the promise of some clerical work. She imagined he knew everything about her, the husband she had left – for no good reason, as everyone believed – how she should return to him, to the home she had abandoned, and right now perhaps be preparing the evening meal or doing the laundry. And what of him, the husband who had suffered this humiliation?

Ellis never intended to carry the guilty burden of Vince with her, especially not this day when she was looking for a new position, and before she lost all control she picked up the unopened folder at which Clive had not even glanced. It contained some sketches and tracing work she'd compiled over a few months. He disappeared back behind the pile of boxes and she walked to the front door, pausing to get her sunglasses out again. She had only just acquired these sunglasses. They were round, outsized, with dark brown frames. She had tried them on one day when waiting for her father to finish an appointment at the optician in Liverpool Road. When she looked into the mirror above the sunglasses display she saw a woman who looked different. With her thick tousled hair and her pearlescent lipstick, there was a hint of glamour. Her father had come out and almost whistled, saying she looked like Jackie Kennedy, and insisted on buying them for her.

It was the first time she had approached a place like this for work, out of the blue. She may as well continue being adventurous. She could return home crushed or she could go farther along King Street. It was early afternoon, the sun was bright.

As she stepped out the door the man in the visor appeared behind her.

'You could, you know.'

'Could what?' she said.

'Create a new word.'

19

¶ WHAT OF CHARLIE? DOVE HAD NOT forgotten him, but every time she tried to turn her mind to the story of Charlie, after Ellis left the child with Vince and commenced what amounted to another life, she could not work it out.

Being a novelist was so hard. She wondered if she really had chosen to do what she was doing, or if some unseen force had sneaked up on her and possessed her and forced her into it. One thing it involved was something that, had Dove foreseen it, meant she would have tried with all her might to turn her back on it. She would have remained a graphic designer, albeit a reluctant one in an unhappy work situation. This was sharing the emotional agony of her characters. Surely it was not meant to be like this, surely they should not have the power to distress her the way they did.

And what had happened to Charlie could only be distressing. Though for him the consequences were not nearly so bad, in fact it seemed to Dove that she had suffered far more for knowing and now writing about Charlie's story than he did himself.

She had not meant to write the story of women but that was how it had appeared, that was the only story in her head. The more she delved into the lives of her characters the more it was about missing or silent women and the more it seemed it was her job to find them and open their mouths and pull their words out and lay them across the pages. Ellis had stepped out of a longer story, one in which women were always grasping for some sense of authenticity, and in which mothers in particular were absent. *Wuthering Heights* had almost no mothers and certainly none whom you could say were good to any degree. They were all dead or dying, or simply blank spaces, unnamed and unacknowledged, as if their progeny – Heathcliff, Catherine, Hindley, Edgar, Nelly – had been produced by magic, or had just sprung up out of the earth like the primaeval rocks or heather that spread across the windy moors.

Dove remembered that Charlie was born in the late 1960s and would by now, at the time she was writing, have been a man in his late forties, eight or ten years older than she. She began to fantasise about Charlie, imagining him as an older friend, or perhaps a brother, which of course she had never had.

All her childhood, and well past it, Dove had fantasised about having siblings in the way that only children often do.

When she was younger she had vacillated between resentment at being an only child and smugness at the privilege of it. One of her friends was the eldest of five children and shared a bedroom with her two sisters, a tiny room where books and clothes were fought over and private space stoutly defended. When she and Dove were in their first year of high school, they barricaded the door one afternoon to examine their Personal Development handouts featuring diagrams of the female internal organs. Only a month or so later Dove waited outside the toilet door while Jenny took her time, groaning and flushing repeatedly. When she emerged she looked pale and pulled at her crotch. 'I don't think it's in properly,' she whispered, although Dove had handed over the leaflet that came with the packet of Meds from which she had furnished Jenny with a tampon, all the while fending off incursions from the giggling younger sisters who demanded to know why they were taking so long in the toilet. Fortunately the little brothers were parked in front of the television watching the afternoon cartoons. Jenny's mother, who was a Catholic and had odd views, had given her daughter a packet of bulky pads with sticky backs that were meant to stay in place, but somehow worked themselves free. All Jenny's mother had said to her daughter on the topic of menstruation was about keeping the packets out of sight and disposing of the used ones discreetly in the bin. When Dove had told her mother, Jane had snorted. 'Is it still 1950?' she'd said. 'The poor girl. Tell her to come to me if she wants any help, although god knows with all these ads on the telly a girl needn't be ignorant these days.'

At times like this Dove was not only glad she had no siblings, but also that she had a mother who was so sensible, so straightforward, who seemed unfazed by menstruation or teenage boys or late-night phone calls or all the erratic adolescent habits that gave Jenny's mother so much anxiety. Now and then she would phone Jane to elicit sympathy, about Jenny's failure to return from a party by the approved hour, or the fact that she seemed to be meeting a boy after school in secret, or that she had smelled cigarettes on her, when it was about to become illegal for children under sixteen to purchase them! After these conversations, in which Jane spoke in monosyllables and raised her eyebrows at Dove, she would just sigh and shake her head and return to her book, or music. For Jane childhood was never the catastrophe that others made out, but then – and this took many years for Dove to work out – perhaps that was because Dove never needed to compete for attention and never felt the constraint of rules that demanded to be challenged.

At other times she desperately yearned for a soul mate, a sister or brother who knew you well enough to be almost part of you, in spite of the fact that you might fight like crazy with them.

It was not only her reading of *Wuthering Heights* – for soul mates were clearly also prone to being toxic – but many others that taught her as a child that only children were somehow doomed. Dove knew that the reason she found it hard to make friends was because she and her mother had formed such a tight unit when she was young, and that she instinctively shied from close bonds with anyone because in the back of her mind was always the thought that her mother was there for her. She doubted this would have been so if she had been obliged to share her mother with anyone.

She and Jenny remained friendly enough after they both left school, but after Dove returned from a long overseas trip to find Jenny moved, then married, then a mother of two, there didn't seem to be any point. Someone at Jane's funeral had said to her, 'Don't be a loner now that she's gone. Don't be alone because you're an only child, and adopted.'

No, thought Dove, I'm a loner and alone because I live in my head. Was she, she often asked herself, writing about a woman who had not known her mother because in one way it paralleled her own experience? Only after Jane died did Dove properly confront the absence of a father in her life. She astonished herself, at the age of thirty-eight, when she realised she had barely been bothered by it all her life. She astonished herself even further when on reflection she realised she was not especially curious, even then, to learn what had happened to him. She had supposed that when she went through her mother's things after her death there would be some information, but she found nothing. Well before the stroke that was the beginning of the end, Jane had cleared out all the superfluous paperwork in her spare room and reduced her files to one box that contained copies of their birth certificates – her own simply containing Jane's name, and no father – the deeds to her flat, the registration and insurance papers for her car, which Dove now drove. She had thrown out cards and letters and other tributes, even her teaching certificate and several awards she had received as the music mistress at the private girls' school near Bathurst, a career that had ended after Dove arrived. This life had left no clues, as if there were secrets. The most interesting item was the copy of *Wuthering Heights* that she had first read, with annotations in her mother's and then in her own hand, from when she was a teenager.

If that was the only clue then Dove had to make the most of it, though even after all this time she could not begin to comprehend the reasons this novel set in the bleak Yorkshire landscape had any bearing on her life as an urban woman in the mid-2010s. But one thing was very clear: in *Wuthering Heights* children were as much a necessity as they were a burden. Without them there was no story. Heathcliff and Cathy formed a bond as children, one that could not withstand the advent of adulthood. Cathy, barely out of her teens, died in childbirth, and her daughter Catherine became a loose piece rattling around in the generational box puzzle that formed the story of the novel. None of the children's mothers survived to guide them, and the fathers that did proved to be neglectful, tyrannical or weak.

Was it the story of miserable childhood? Or the story of inept and failed parents? Right at the very start of the novel Dove could see how Mr Earnshaw had erred in his duties by bringing back from his trip to Liverpool a wild nameless boy, instead of the whip and the violin he'd promised his children. And he compounded his failures by setting his son and his adopted son against each other, then dying to leave the bad blood between them like poison brewing in a cauldron. The romantic view promoted a reading about unfettered childhood, roaming free and wild amid nature, thumbing its nose at everything that adulthood supposedly represented, but every time Dove re-read the book she could find none of this: nothing that Cathy and Heathcliff ever did was untainted. There was no such thing as their childhood innocence. And as for the cosy sight towards the end of the novel, where the younger Catherine was teaching the rough-hewn Hareton his letters, this disturbed her greatly, though she could not quite put her finger on what it was. It was not exactly the smug benevolence of Nelly, who somehow survived everyone in the story, nor the foolishness of Lockwood for whom at the very end the sight of two lovers returning from an evening ramble on the moors was unbearable. It was a growing sense that every single character was trapped in the narrative and that it did not matter that three generations were ushered in and out of the story, no one seemed able to escape the tyranny of being alive. And yet, perversely, almost everyone was doomed to die young.

20

―――

⟪ KING STREET WAS A STRANGE BUT exciting place. Cheap diners were next door to second-hand clothing shops and there were endless places selling junk or bric-a-brac. Ellis stopped and peered into the window of one. Green, amber and pink glassware was piled up haphazardly along with Bakelite ashtrays and floral teacups and embroidered linen napkins. It was all the familiar stuff that had surrounded her at home, the stuff that stifled her as a teenager and which she had packed away into the dining room sideboard. Useless, depressing and dust-gathering. There was a tin Negro figure with its hand out, a money box: if one paced a coin in the hand and pressed the lever the hand would lift and the coin would slip into the mouth. There was a tarnished silver coffee and tea service, a set of cut-glass and silver condiment bottles in a silver holder, also tarnished grey. There were vases bearing peacock feathers and stems of dry pampas grass flowers. She hated all that ornamental clutter. Further inside were small items of furniture, chrome and black glass smokers' friends, veneer writing desks, nests of side tables with barley-stick legs, an oak planter with a pot plant that looked like an aspidistra on top. She shuddered. How could people want to buy this stuff, how could they want to surround themselves with this dark dreary furniture, with such clichéd plants?

Perhaps she just found it more depressing than usual. She turned and walked past a chemist shop and a dusty newsagency, an even dustier art store with faded prints and rolls of cardboard in the window display. Past a second-hand bookshop she came to a corner wine bar, a tiny place. If she entered the bookshop she would be trapped for ages. She checked her wristwatch. She didn't need to be heading home for another hour at least.

She had never entered a wine bar before. Now she pushed her way through the swinging louvre doors and sat down at the first table. The place was almost empty. Each table held an empty chianti bottle in a raffia base bearing a stub of red candle, already lit as the place was dark and virtually windowless. The bottle at her table was palaeolithic with layers of wax that had dribbled down the sides. Above her was a dropped ceiling made of lattice, from which dangled more empty bottles tied by their necks with string, and bunches of plastic grapes with leaves trailing along the lattice. She should have a wine, but was not interested in ordering a sherry, which was the only wine she'd ever really drunk. Her father drank spirits, whisky and brandy with soda, and Vince had only drunk beer, and aside from that no one around her much had drunk. The fellowship group had frowned on all liquor, although she knew that some of them enjoyed a quiet drink and cigarette when separated from the pack. And the women she'd known, at parties or barbecues, drank things like Pimm's with lemonade or shandies or punch, and all those drinks were far too sweet. In her final year of school a girl had somehow acquired a bottle of Barossa Pearl which was passed around along with a packet of Craven As one Saturday night behind the library block. In the dark she had nearly missed the mouth of the bottle when it came her way and then wanted to spit the wine out, it was that warm and sweet. Two of the girls proceeded to giggle and sway as they made their way back to the dormitory. Ellis was convinced they could not be drunk but one of them claimed to be ill the next morning. 'Hangover,' she had whispered proudly, pulling the sheets up to her chin to avoid the mistress rostered on to chase them out of bed and off to morning service.

She picked up a narrow menu in a plastic folder. Nothing on the list was familiar. Most of the wines were French or Italian and she was having trouble working out which were red and which were white and then realised she could probably only order a whole bottle, which she would never drink. She felt stupid and faintly panicky. And she had no idea what she liked. No idea at all. Fortunately, a couple had entered and headed straight to the bar at the end of the room. That would give her time to escape.

'Yippie.'

'Pardon?'

'Yippie,' he repeated, leaning over her table. It was the man from the printer's shop. He had removed the visor. 'May I sit here?'

She barely nodded but he pulled out a chair anyway.

'I'm sorry,' she said. 'I don't know what you mean.'

He was smiling as he picked up the menu and ran his eyes up and down the list, flipped it over, then tossed it down.

'You were saying you couldn't invent a new word. There's one for you, just a year or two old. A baby of a word. No, a toddler.' He laughed.

'What does it mean?' Ellis stiffened. He was laughing at her. And now she was revealing her ignorance. She picked up the menu he had dropped. She could order a bottle of anything and pretend to like it or not, then walk off and leave it, if she wanted.

Possibly he sensed her discomfort. He held out his hand. 'Thomas Sanders,' he said. 'But call me Tom.'

She took it and he grasped hers firmly. Another first: she didn't recall ever being shaken by the hand. That was the sort of thing men always did. She told him her name.

'You don't mind me dropping in? I finished work early. I hope you didn't think I was following you. But you were fantastic, back in the factory. Old Clive didn't know what hit him. No woman has ever fronted up and asked for a job like that. Especially not someone smart and glamorous.'

Ellis glowed and squirmed at the same time. She knew she was meant to be pleased but she wished she wasn't being complimented.

'This word, yippie. Is it in the dictionary?'

He caught her eye. 'Probably not. It means a member of the Youth International Party. Big in America, not so well known here. We did some posters for them last year. I don't think there was much of a turnout for their rally.'

He talked about the counterculture, about writers and artists. Abbie Hoffman and Jerry Rubin and Paul Krassner and Alan Ginsberg. He moved on to demonstrations against governments and the need to liberate youth, about the oppression caused by capitalism and religions, and the importance of peace. He stopped to ask if she was having a drink, and she made a gesture signifying anything, too preoccupied with all he had told her. He went to the bar and returned with a carafe of red wine and two glasses.

'Claret,' he said succinctly. 'Only the house stuff, but it's okay.'

He was acting to impress. She suspected he was nervous under an exterior that implied intimate knowledge of wines and even more intimate acquaintance with this bar in particular. She would not reveal any more of her ignorance but simply took a sip. Immediately she liked the dry taste, the richness of it. Meanwhile her head was abuzz. He had mentioned people and the sort of ideas that barely filtered through to her little suburban world. She knew it was a conservative existence, and there was nothing she could do about it. Her father didn't even much like reading the newspapers these days. But this man, well, doubtless he had something to do with the university, and went on demonstrations, and read radical magazines. He probably printed them. Maybe that was why he was so knowledgeable. She had never heard of a yippie. Presumably it was a variation of a hippie.

'You know,' he said, comfortably picking up the topic of conversation, 'people are being persecuted here for smoking pot, while over in Vietnam they're being burned to death or blown up. Does that make sense?'

Of course it did not make sense. No sane person could agree that it did, put like that. But Ellis would not mention that her ex-husband's brother had served there. Tom seemed to be waiting for an answer. She looked closer at him. Despite the dim light she could see grey strands in his curls. He would be several years older than she.

'You haven't fought?'

'Conscientious objector,' he said. 'Got picked in one of the birthday ballots six years ago.'

That made him about twenty-six. He looked older.

'Hardly anyone objected then, not like now. Or if they did it wasn't reported much,' he said.

She never recalled hearing anyone protesting about the war in the first few years.

'Were you jailed?'

'Cops picked me up a few times but I kept moving around. Laid low until they finally left me alone. And I had a good lawyer.'

Maybe Ellis was not against the war – that was a complex issue, best left to the country in question, and she would not pretend to understand that – but she didn't see why Australia belonged there.

'The sooner we get out of there the better,' she said, the heat in her voice surprising even her. It was the first time she had spoken such a thought aloud. In the past few years she had hardly dared to have an opinion on anything, let alone voice it. But she believed it.

He held her gaze for a second. She picked up her glass and drank another mouthful. He took out his cigarettes and reached over to grab an ashtray from the next table.

'What words would you invent?' he said after lighting up.

Ellis thought for a moment. Imagine inventing language, wasn't that what other people did? Old men in wood-panelled rooms somewhere, Oxford or Cambridge, sitting over their pipes and glasses of port and shuffling around piles of books and notes. But of course, now that Tom had posed the question, it made sense: language was mobile, shifting. And democratic. It was not as if there was some law that said an ordinary person couldn't have a hand in it.

'When I was a kid,' he continued, 'my little brother couldn't pronounce cutlery: he called it cluttery. We started calling the kitchen drawer that gets full of all the bits and pieces the cluttery drawer. It kind of stuck.'

She didn't know if it was the benign image of the drawer that she knew straightaway, indeed could see in her mind, for they had one at home – cluttered with odd rubber bands and skewers and corkscrews and unpaired knives and forks, along with cookie cutters and napkin rings and the knife steel – or if it was just a perfect term, but she warmed to the idea, and to him.

'That should definitely be in the dictionary,' she said.

'What about you?'

'Nothing I've ever invented, even when I was a kid. But I read a book recently that had a new word in it. Nymphet. And faunlet. I liked that.'

'Really?' He smiled. 'I was working for a bookshop for a while. Just farther up the road here. We made a fortune posting that book off to customers in Victoria. You know it was banned down there? Probably still is.'

'Yes, I know.'

It had taken ages to persuade Miss Neville to lend her a copy. She got the impression that the library had obtained it only very reluctantly, and that if Miss Neville had had any say in it, then *Lolita* would never have debased the collection of Ashfield library at all. There was apparently a waiting list to read it, but Ellis had not been convinced. She spent a lot of time in the library and had never encountered anyone asking for the book. After weeks of polite questioning and being told it was on loan to someone, Miss Neville had finally produced it from a cupboard in the office behind the loans desk. One week, she had said, stamping the card harder than necessary and ferreting around for a paper bag. She had handed it over to Ellis holding it by her fingertips, as if mere brown paper could not protect her from the filth inside.

'Have you read it?' Ellis had asked her, somewhat mischievously, to be told emphatically of course not. Why she had wondered, was there this special breed of righteous librarians, mostly female, with the self-appointed task of guarding the morals of the suburbs? Miss Neville was like a younger, thinner version of dour Muriel Curry, her ex mother-in-law, who had held the same suspicion of novels, any novels, as she had of hard liquor, dancing and women who wore red shoes. After *Lolita*, Ellis knew her relationship with the librarian had changed forever.

'What about you?' she said. 'What exactly do you do at the printery?'

'Just routine stuff, part time. A lot of proofreading for Clive. But I love typefaces too, you know. They tell amazing stories.'

'Yes,' she said. 'That's what I thought too!' She leaned back, feeling she had been too enthusiastic, but Tom seemed not to notice.

'Do you know, there's this strange story about a drowned typeface.'

She shook her head, she didn't know it. He went on to describe the beautifully flawed typeface that was lost after being thrown into a river. It had been used to print a King James Bible in the early twentieth century, and nothing more. Its bookbinder owner was unwilling to pass the type on to his partner and so threw the entire stock from a bridge into the River Thames. Night after night, for months until it was all consigned to the water and the mud, Edward Cobden-Sanderson tossed heavy blocks of type, as many as he could manage – for he was elderly – from the Hammersmith Bridge, fearing detection but never being caught.

It was a haunting thought. 'Why did he do that?' she said.

'No one really knows. Clearly it meant something more to him, so much that he sacrificed it forever.'

Ellis felt inexplicably saddened by this story. She stood up. 'I must go,' she said.

'Before you do,' Tom said, 'the reason I dropped by when I saw you come in here.'

'Yes?'

'Well, I remembered, after you left the print shop. There's this job going, at one of the magazines. I do some freelance work for them. You might want to follow it up.'

He handed her a card, on which he'd written his name and a phone number.

'Call me if you're interested. I could introduce you to the editor if you like.'

21

⊂ WUTHERING: THAT WAS A MADE-UP word, surely? Dove had researched it and could find no instance of the term before 1846. Wuthering was a true neologism, one that Emily Brontë fashioned from the local dialect, or at the very least had been the first to offer in print. Just mouthing the word she could feel the tremendous roaring of the wind, the icy blast that enveloped those caught and exposed in it, the elemental force that penetrated coats and cloaks, ear muffs and gloves, and sent people searching desperately for shelter. It was a wild, mongrel, wilful sort of word, one that was unpindownable. Terrifying and exhilarating at the same time.

There was another powerful word, not exactly a neologism, but certainly one that was new to Ellis's world, and Dove could see this word forming in the back of her mind. Feminism, and as she typed it she felt the power of that word. She lived in post-feminist times supposedly, where liberal, spirited, independent women spurned the term as something linked to irrelevancies like the arguments over high heels or leg shaving, or rallies for equal pay. In only another year or two Ellis would be calling herself a feminist and dealing with all the compromises of being personally empowered, progressive and open-minded, but in a work context that was only slowly catching up – indeed at times it would seem not to be moving at all. Being in the world where this word was making its impact felt was, for women like Ellis, sometimes disorienting. Power often was. Or in her case, empowerment, which was not the same thing. Dove understood that much.

And she understood that something frightening was about to happen. Something liberating but frightening, and as she thought about it – and thought again about the maddening autonomy these characters exerted, well beyond her control – she believed she began to understand the author of *Wuthering Heights* a tiny bit more. Emily Brontë never compromised in her portrayal of Heathcliff and Cathy. Perhaps her sister Charlotte was actually correct when she claimed that having formed these beings Emily did not know what she had done. Or maybe she had, and resolutely refused to reflect on the implications – moral, artistic – of these creations, but let them be who they needed to be. In which case Charlotte was also right when she remarked that her sister would have wondered why anyone would complain about the relentless, implacable and disturbing natures depicted in her novel, about the spirits so lost and fallen that certain fearful scenes prevented a reader from sleeping at night.

Could Dove, however, exert the same pitiless inexorable spirit as the author of *Wuthering Heights*? When she thought about what had happened already, and what was going to happen in her story, she felt profoundly disturbed, so much so that she knew there were scenes she felt she was not going to be brave enough to write. In one of these scenes that loomed like a film trailer, teasing and unresolved, she saw Ellis at an interview for the magazine, and understood the exciting prospect of the position, understood that Ellis, still young, had immense talent and that the position would nurture much in her, a particular feel for the magazine industry that combined creativity with hard-headed business skills. Ellis was poised at a moment in time where a whole generation of people, women and men, but clearly mainly young women, would finally slough off the first half of the century, escape the much-lauded postwar boom years and embrace their future.

But the cost. Dove considered the scene as it unfolded in more detail and knew she would write it in one way, despite her misgivings. Two scenes in particular, and the idea of them so forceful that no one would recognise the Ellis who had not so long ago been soaking her husband's greasy work clothes or preparing his favourite dishes, even if she disliked them. Or who visited her father every week to help him around the house, when she had a baby to care for.

They would recognise her, she supposed, if they kept in mind that she was a woman who married too young and not for love, who at the time believed it was the only role available to her, and who was trying to atone for something she believed was entirely her fault. Above all, they would recognise the actions of a woman who had never known her own mother and whose life thus was and always would be undermined by the terrible loss, indeed a tragedy that claimed her from the start. They would understand this was a woman who went through life with the wind forever whistling through a space in her chest.

Wuthering. The wind had always wuthered in Ellis's heart, no matter how hard at times she could pretend all was sunny.

22

⸦ ON HER FIRST DAY ELLIS WAS GIVEN THE job of sorting through recipes that readers submitted for publication. The best each month won a prize of a year's subscription to the magazine. The deputy editor made it clear that it was a relief to relinquish this insulting task.

'If we had a proper cookery editor,' she said, 'then I wouldn't have had to think about it at all.'

Valerie was tall with bold dyed red hair, her body draped in silk scarves, and she wore cork-soled sandals that clattered dramatically as she strode out of the lift each morning.

She handed Ellis a cardboard box of letters and returned to her desk to blow menthol-scented smoke into the air as she shouted into the phone. Periodically the photography director would saunter over to perch on her desk and they would laugh like lunatics.

When the test kitchen sent up plates of pinwheel sandwiches or upside-down cakes or chocolate mousse in coffee cups, Valerie would wave him and the fashion editor over first, before inviting the lesser mortals in the office to sample the leftovers.

The first winning recipe Ellis selected was for chicken casserole Italienne, cooked in a clay dish called a Schlemmertopf. It was the first time she had come across a recipe that called for so much garlic, and she had never heard of a Schlemmertopf. Most of the recipes submitted were dismal. Novelty ways with minced meat. French onion soup dip. A spicy lamb dish that sounded interesting but went on to feature gingernut biscuits, of all things, that you were meant to soak in boiling water. When she showed Valerie her choice, the deputy editor wrinkled her nose and said, 'I don't think so. Where on earth would readers find a Schlemmertopf?'

So Ellis chose instead a recipe for a foolproof lemon meringue pie. There was nothing exciting about a lemon meringue pie, in her view; however the reader had understood the importance of using fresh lemons, to ensure the lemon base set correctly, and she knew this was true: Mrs Wood had always made their lemon butter using fresh fruit from their tree in the back garden. 'If you buy lemons,' she said, 'you don't know how old they are.' The winning reader wrote her a letter of gratitude.

The magazine's full title was the *Women's Pages*. But they all called it the *Pages*, and Valerie explained the name would soon be official, with the revamp. New sections, new cover design and so on. She hinted smokily from a narrowed mouth that she was pretty much opposed to all this since the magazine did very nicely as it was, and that the new editor who'd come on board only a few months earlier was throwing his weight around far too much. He didn't understand that the position was more of an executive one, that the magazine had always been her thing. Soon she was confiding in Ellis, in short quiet bursts of conversation when she passed her desk. Ellis understood this was part of her breaking-in process. And that she would probably soon be forced to take sides.

'Everyone knows that this editor,' Valerie said, refusing to use his name, 'has no experience in the business. But what can you expect from a guy who only got the job because he's gone to the same private school as the publisher's son?'

Ellis murmured something inoffensive. She hadn't heard of any of these people.

'And you know, my greatest success,' Valerie leaned closer to Ellis for this piece of information, 'has been making this middlebrow household magazine appeal across the board.'

That was true enough. Ellis had already done her research and knew that despite its name and content, the *Pages* turned out to be read by a surprising number of men.

A few weeks after commencing, sifting through hand-written recipes – every week someone seemed to think that deep fried camembert was the most inventive dish they'd heard of – Ellis was wondering how to appear to be busier than she was. The various test kitchen dishes she'd sampled seemed deeply unexciting. For all Valerie's boasting and flamboyance, the magazine was unexciting and predictable, as far as she could determine. In her spare time, and there was plenty, she looked through past issues and noted how often the same subjects were recycled: features on rock gardens or tie-dying received new photo shoots but not much else. Valerie boasted that the *Pages* contained current affairs but in fact these were profiles of politicians' wives, safely offered in the same format, always ending with their list of favourite foods, favourite piece of furniture and favourite holiday destinations. The fashion editor rarely appeared at work before noon, and already several times Ellis had been asked to help set up shoots in the little studio, getting the models dressed and running around scouring makeshift props, so they could meet deadlines.

The job she eyed, from her assistant's desk in the corner of the open-plan office, was that of the woman who was sent off to interview celebrities and arty types. She commanded the most thrilling authority, being able to slam her phone down with satisfaction and announce to the room that she'd nabbed an exclusive with Bob and Dolly Dyer, or this playwright that everyone was talking about, David Williamson, before snapping her fingers for a photographer and marching out into the real world of culture and personalities.

'There'll be a lot more of that too,' Valerie hinted one day when she brushed past Ellis's desk as she was proofreading the winter soups supplement. Apparently, if the editor had his way, there would be more of what she derided as highbrow arty stuff.

Occasionally Valerie's phone call bark became a whimper as she responded to a call from upstairs. She would disappear before lunch and when she returned, huddle in with the photography director for the rest of the afternoon, both of them swathed in cigarette smoke.

The magazine's more sophisticated revamp somehow sat uneasily with Valerie's style. She continued to manage but refused to be enthusiastic about its fresher layout, its uncluttered feature articles. The fact that the puzzles and games were relegated to the very back of the magazine, and soon banished forever, she seemed to take personally. Ellis wondered if it was as simple as two bold, extravagant personalities competing, if Valerie had somehow shone brighter when the magazine was a more humble entity featuring photo spreads of cute kids and animals with punning captions.

One day the editor refused to approve the feature she'd done on Mrs Whitlam, claiming it was trivial and boring. The pasted-up pages came back downstairs and they all had to stay at work late putting together something to substitute.

'He said he wanted more substance,' she grumbled. 'Less about her curtains and more about her being a social worker, or something.' She sniffed to show the extent of her interest in Mrs Whitlam's previous career.

'She is an interesting woman, though,' Ellis ventured. Valerie threw her a look and marched back to her desk.

It was the same look that Ellis remembered catching years ago from those women at Betty Denman's place when she'd said she admired Ainsley Gotto. Perhaps people like Valerie, for all their boldness and appearance of independence, hadn't really twigged that things had changed, were changing every day. Or they did understand and didn't like it. The Whitlams had copped a lot of criticism, especially Margaret whose dress style was now being unfavourably compared with Sonia McMahon's, but Ellis felt quite giddy when she thought of them. Suddenly she had a new understanding of this place, a sense of the whole country shifting around, resettling in a newer, stronger position, with these tall god-like creatures in charge. She thought about Australia as an idea now, a possibility, in a way that she'd never thought about the country before. And her place in it, however minuscule.

Within a year, Valerie took extended leave. The day before she was due to return to work, a telex arrived announcing she had decided to remain in London, where she'd met someone.

The editor appeared in the office with a frown. He too was leaving for another position and the person who had been filling in for Valerie was going off to have a baby at the end of the week.

'Would you like a chocolate truffle?' Ellis said, holding out a plate that she'd just brought up from the test kitchen. She had made some at home the week before and suggested the kitchen try them.

He looked dazed, but took one.

'Delicious. Did you make them?'

'Yes,' she said. And it was almost true.

*

ELLIS'S TEMPORARY PROMOTION soon became permanent. She came in to work early and left late, and when the new managing editor, who worked for the parent company, made comments about women being unreliable, always disappearing to follow lovers or have babies, she made sure she kept her mouth shut.

The magazine sold and sold, and soon the days of editing the cookery and craft sections of the *Women's Pages*, with its crochet patterns and recipes for devilled sausages, seemed a laughable distant past. As deputy editor she had much autonomy. She introduced restaurant reviews and more interviews with artists, musicians and actors. The social pages stopped covering weddings in the eastern suburbs and charity balls and now featured the crowds at gallery openings, first nights of plays, and the interesting types who gathered in Balmain pubs discussing books and politics. The women's pages, in her mind, were still represented in the re-formed magazine, and always would be; but instead they included profiles of prominent women and featured more articles on social issues than domestic ones. They had published an interview with Germaine Greer and followed it up in the next issue with an article about women lawyers. The features editor was planning a long piece on adoption, and anonymous interviews with women whose babies had been taken away.

But Ellis was not fooled. By the mid-1970s she was not secure enough in her position to imagine that there was really such a thing as equality, despite what everyone was saying. Some time in the middle of that decade she was required to make a choice. She stood in the office of the vice-president and executive editor. In a couple of years several of the many progeny of the parent company had merged, and the consequent restructure meant the vice-president had more control over each. He was a cliché, a cigar-chewing, pot-bellied man with a cheery geniality that barely cloaked his contempt. In his world, several floors above that of the *Pages*, women like Ellis were always implicitly undergoing some sort of test. He was planning to promote her from deputy to editor.

'This,' he said, 'means you can take full charge and steer the magazine into a newer, more exciting direction. Should you choose.'

It was implied she would not fail to choose.

'It's only a few years since you've joined us,' he reminded her. 'I can see you're still young but quick to learn. And full of potential.' He leaned back in his chair and plugged his mouth with the cigar.

She didn't seem to be required to speak, beyond muttering the occasional yes and thanks. It was a great step for her. Finally she did say something.

'I'm honoured. And grateful.'

'No need for that,' he said. 'But you do need to understand that this trust in your capabilities deserves some loyalty in return.'

The vice-president took a considered chew of his cigar. He was the kind of man who rarely lit up but was usually rolling one around in his hands, taking it out of his mouth and jabbing it for emphasis. He did this now, pointing at Ellis. He didn't mean loyalty to him, mind you, that was not what he expected. He meant to the company. If she were to accept this offer – and really, was there any doubt that she would; he was simply running through the formalities for the sheer pleasure of savouring the power it gave him, just like the cigar in his mouth – then he would expect in return nothing but her absolute commitment. He'd need her to remain at the helm and guide the magazine through its crucial years of change, and of course she could take the odd holiday but it needed to be understood – he jabbed again with the cigar, right at her belly now – that none of this nonsense about running off to get married or taking time out to look after babies would be tolerated.

Ellis, as was perhaps correct, was standing before her seated employer. He liked to work in his shirtsleeves with a loosened tie to suggest that despite the continent of inlaid maple between them and the submarine cigar berthed in his mouth, he was only one of the workers at heart.

She swallowed the humiliation at having her body accused, as it were, and at being made to stand and be accountable for all modern women who dared to have a career and who might betray the great faith their male employers were starting to put in them by being weak enough to fall in love, or to have children. Despite the acid shame and faint dread inside her, Ellis remained steady and focused, holding the vice-president's gaze as she stood. As if deliberately, she smoothed down her skirt over her still flat stomach and then reached out over the desk to shake his hand.

'You have nothing to worry about,' she said. 'You can count on my cooperation one hundred per cent.'

The smile remained on her face as, head erect, she walked across the executive level and down two flights of stairs back to the editorial and production floor, where she went straight to her own desk. At lunchtime, when the office was quiet, she picked up the phone and called Tom.

23

———

❡ DOVE UNDERSTOOD HOW WOMEN WERE discriminated against. She had lived through some of that herself. Though she could not claim that the few incidents had seriously violated her, not really, not when atrocities were committed against women, the memory of the student coffee lounge where Jabe had groped her breast was still raw. But she had never experienced what women like Ellis had experienced.

Nevertheless, she did not know how Ellis could do that, how she displayed such an implacable spirit. It seemed nothing short of callous. She saw her speaking quietly into the phone, then resuming work and not leaving until the normal time. She saw Tom arriving at Ellis's flat about an hour later, heard the argument that went on, a muted one for neither was prone to scenes or shouting. She saw Tom on the balcony smoking cigarette after cigarette, throwing the butts into the stand of palms that formed the tiny front garden of the block of flats in the main street of Potts Point, where Ellis now lived, without caring who might be below, or even if they might land farther out on the footpath. She saw him walk out, then return, then walk out again. And she saw Ellis, the very next day, telephone to tell work she would be in a little later, then make a few more calls before heading off herself. This morning, she wore a peasant top over a camisole, a floral skirt and brown boots. Around her neck was a lace choker and her hair, which she now wore permed, was piled into a pleasing mess. The magazine was featuring fashions popularised by Yves St Laurent, and while Ellis rarely took samples the fashion editor offered, she had decided she liked this new look. She was vastly different to the Ellis of just a few years before, in velour jersey scoop-neck tops and flared jeans, or the Ellis of the late 1960s, a lookalike Mary Quant in miniskirts and patterned tights, her hair short and sleek as a fur seal.

On this morning, Ellis took the bus to work as usual but everything was so different that Dove would not have been surprised if the bus turned out to be painted purple or sparkly pink instead of blue. Ellis had made a decision from which there could be no going back. Tom could or could not return as he wished. She did not believe that she owed him anything and refused to be disproportionately grateful just because it was he who had introduced her to the position at the magazine, and her whole career, five or six years ago. She was the one who had carried it through, become successful, done the hard work.

When she arrived at the office she phoned the personnel department and straight after morning tea went up to the seventh floor for a meeting, then went the next floor up to the executive level and knocked on the door of the vice-president's secretary and insisted on a meeting straightaway.

Dove was astonished. Ellis virtually barged into the inner sanctum, where the vice-president, again in shirtsleeves and unwrapping his first cigar of the day, half rose in his chair, then sat back, mouth slightly open, as he listened to Ellis. The executive offices were panelled in beautiful Queensland maple, with glass partitions rising from waist height to the ceiling. Next to the vice-president's office was another even larger one, with an ensuite and drinks cabinet and a one-hundred-and-ninety-degree view of the city, but which was left empty in memory of his father who had started the company and who would always remain the president, at least so long as his son was around. On the father's vast desk sat a silver tray with decanter and a crystal tumbler which the secretary renewed every morning at eleven o'clock, with two fingers of Scotch whisky and five cubes of ice. At the patriarch's home there were similar rituals, regarded by everyone – the rest of the family, their circle of friends, along with anyone else who happened to be in the know – with indulgence as the endearing eccentricities of the wealthy and powerful classes. For example, a place was always set for him at dinner, his widow sitting to the left, his eldest son the vice-president to his right, and at these dinners, whether grand events or private family meals, three things were never served, for the patriarch had hated them: carrots, in any form; apple sauce, even when there was roast pork; and hard boiled eggs, with their ugly grey rims surrounding the yolk.

All this information was but a maddening distraction to Dove who was trying to tune into the conversation unfolding before her, but it was as if they were behind thick impenetrable glass that allowed vision but nothing else. Ellis, she feared, was taking a huge risk but one that might pay off, for it would show the vice-president, sexist bully that he was, that she was a person of firmness and decisiveness, who was as prepared as he was to insist on deals and barter with people's lives, in return for results. In his parlance, she was showing she had balls. If he agreed to her proposal she would not let him down. But at the end of her five-minute lecture – which is what it looked like to Dove, Ellis even at one stage placing her hands on her hips – he was sitting back in his chair, his lips pressed shut around the cigar, his eyebrows knitted. And she was holding her chin high, still refusing to sit down. By lunchtime it was all arranged. And when Ellis returned to her desk on the sixth floor and sat down again it was like a film come abruptly to an end.

Dove raked over all that she could see, sifting it for details. She knew that Ellis had also made a phone call to someone in the country, but she had no idea who they were or where they were. And all she understood from the meetings at Ellis's work was that management had agreed she could take her accumulated leave in one chunk a little later in the year. After that the scene simply stopped. No credits, nothing. She had no idea what would come next, or even if she would be allowed to witness it.

24

⸿ ELLIS HAD NEVER LEARNED TO DRIVE, AS it happened. She had intended to, but after she left Vince, left her father's place and moved to the inner city, there was nowhere she could not reach by bus or train, or taxi, and the years went past until she was nearing her thirties and there seemed no point.

This time she was travelling by taxi. She paid the driver and got out with some difficulty, adjusting the bundle in a pale yellow shawl in one arm, a bulky overnight bag in the other, and a small shoulder bag. As she walked past the ramp in Eddy Avenue she considered buying a bunch of flowers. The stall had been there for as long as she remembered, and always had something interesting. Sweet peas would have been nice, or poppies. Columbines would have been perfect.

But flowers were impractical. Soon she would be on the train and then it would be several hours before she could hand them over.

She took the escalator up to the country trains and stood before the yellow and black indicator board. Her train was leaving from Platform 4. She had fifteen minutes, not long enough to go and have breakfast. Instead she bought a takeaway coffee in a polystyrene cup and a packet of Smith's Crisps to take onto the train while she waited. The railway pie was considered to be surprisingly good, but she would not risk it, while the look of the doughnuts and finger buns glistening with sugary lacquer made her queasy. But she was starving. In her bag were two apples and a can of Tab, which she had packed at the last minute, and she would save them for later. There were also two small bottles in an insulated bag. She had boiled them sterile and made up hot formula earlier in the morning. Her breasts were still sore and leaking but she had tucked pads into her bra and hooked it looser than usual. In another week or two she should be right, the postnatal sister had advised. Besides, not every woman fed her own baby. In fact she, who had been a midwife since the fifties, could tell Ellis that breastfeeding was only slowly coming back into favour.

She had not contacted Tom. He had been offered a position in Melbourne and would have left anyway if she had not lied and told him she was flying to London to visit relatives and then travel around Europe. She had already lied when she told him she would terminate the pregnancy but she could never do that again. Instead she had booked the hospital and taken her accumulated holiday leave as planned, telling everyone she was off overseas for three months. She phoned her father in the final few weeks instead of visiting him, pleading flu or other reasons. Caftans and other Indian-inspired fashions assisted in the conspiracy. Tom sent a postcard from Melbourne, a picture of the neon Skipping Girl Vinegar sign taken at dusk, which she put in the drawer under the telephone.

The baby was placid. She was the sweetest thing Ellis had ever held. She was perfect yet also unformed, her chest softer than anything but beating with a visible urgent pulse that showed the great strength inside that would make her grow. Out of her tiny mouth her breath issued with a wholesome fragrance. Even when she cried she was as supplicant as a baby bird. Everything about her was startlingly fresh. Ellis could hardly bear it. She resisted holding her for hours on hours, then gathered her up and pressed her close, marvelling at the softness of her cheeks, the down-like gold of her hair, before replacing her in the bassinet and closing the door of the spare room.

It had been two weeks since the birth and she would have left sooner if it could have been arranged, the very next day if at all possible, but she had unexpected complications and required rest. A painful misalignment in her lower back, and some stitches. She had spent five days in hospital then another week confined to home, treating herself with ice and hot water bottles. Getting up the stairs with her hospital bag and the baby had been murder.

After Strathfield she drowsed during the long trip through the western suburbs, the baby tucked into her arms as if it would be there for the rest of her life. At the foothills of the Blue Mountains the baby roused and began making the mild animal squeaks that passed for her cries, and Ellis placed her on the empty seat beside her, changing the disposable nappy and wiping her hands clean with a damp flannel she had prepared and placed in a plastic bag. The baby, settled again in her arms, accepted the teat of the bottle which was still warm. Well before they reached Katoomba she had slipped into sleep again, a small dribble of milk trailing out of her plump wet mouth. Her body was a soft parcel, perfectly compliant within the shape of Ellis's arms. Outside the carriage a drizzle had developed, the kind of soft mist that enveloped the primaeval mountainscape like the innocent infant rain that supposedly descended upon the garden of Eden at night.

The birth had not been as bad as she expected. This time she had read a couple of books which sounded grave and sensible, but when the labour commenced she forgot all the advice she might have gleaned from within their sterile descriptions of what amounted to a force that was more elemental – shocking and exhilarating at the same time – than she anticipated. She had leafed through *A Child Is Born* and marvelled at the insider's view of the being developing within her, changing week by week according to Nilsson's surreal photographs, like something from science fiction. There was not a great deal to read that she found useful. The nurses at the antenatal clinic seemed surprised when she asked for suggestions of books, reassuring her that she would be in safe hands when the time came. Towards the end of the pregnancy she consulted Dr Spock's *The Common Sense Book of Baby and Child Care*, expecting that the early chapters would contain something useful on the event that was about to take place. *Trust yourself*, said the opening lines. *You know more than you think you do.*

She had slapped the book shut then and put it away. She would never know anything. Afterwards, she packed it in the bag and brought it with her along with the rest of the items she had acquired for the baby in the last few weeks.

In the end the birth was over sooner than she expected. Either that or real time suspended while hospital time speeded and skidded to a halt in its own unique manner. She seemed to be watching a nurse sitting in a corner of the delivery ward and reading for hours. But then the same nurse had also been bringing her ice and warm towels and after that never left her side, rubbing her lower back and telling her in a low voice that she was doing really well. Gripped by pain so powerful she could only gasp and moan, lying on her side and panting in between contractions, she succumbed to a dizzy otherworldly state when someone slipped a mask of oxygen over her face. By the time she realised the ridiculous hospital gown was riding up and exposing her backside, the midwife was getting her to sit and draw up her legs. She clutched hard on a pillow placed between her chest and her knees and breathed in and out with extraordinary effort, understanding why it was called labour.

Yet as undeniably corporeal it all was, at the same time she felt detached. In a dream, she was floating above herself and wondering at the curious spectacle of her engorged lower body draped in a green hospital sheet, legs askew, like an enormous bloated praying mantis. And when the midwife pressed on her abdomen and the doctor – it seemed he was conjured up from thin air just minutes before the baby crowned – held up his hands, she was astonished, not that this dripping lumpy sausage was a baby, but that it was her baby.

The train slowed, shuddered, stopped altogether. She looked out the window but it was hard to tell where they were. Paddocks either side of the train, a few indifferent sheep and slicing sheets of rain that replaced the hazy moisture that had accompanied the train all through the mountains and fogged up the windows. But it could not be much farther judging by the time, so she tidied the baby's few things, fastened the overnight bag and put on her jacket.

How and where had her mother gone, when she left? All her life Ellis had wondered why she had disappeared, but now she thought more about the actual event. Had she also gone on a long train trip somewhere, but one so far away that returning was an impossibility? She did not imagine her mother simply patted her on the head and drove off in the back seat of a taxi, or was spirited away by some mysterious person, like in a fairy story. But the most compelling image was of her mother stepping on a train at Central, just as she herself had a few hours ago, and heading west in one long silver journey that spat her out so far at the other edge of the country there could be no coming back. Try as she could, Ellis could never salvage the smallest scrap of memory of that time. She shook her head. She was not doing what her mother had done, only what she needed to do. Drawing a lipstick from her shoulder bag, she coloured her lips and ran her fingers through her hair.

When she got out at the station the sun had broken through but the clouds remained dark and swollen. She had been in the last carriage when the train left, so was at the very end of the platform. She thought she might have to wait and looked up the platform for the waiting room sign, but then a small figure in a dark skirt and coat rose from a seat and walked straight towards her. They stared at each other. Ellis thought if she spoke she might cry. Then she pressed the baby close to her chest before holding her out. The other woman raised her arms and for a few moments there were two sets of hands around the bundle before Ellis stepped back.

I will not kiss her, she thought. I will not touch her again.

'Why don't you come back to my place?'

'No,' she said. 'Thanks. But it's better this way. I am getting the train straight back.' She handed over the bag. 'Everything you need is in there.'

'I understand,' the woman said, bending her face to the baby's exquisite sleeping one.

All of a sudden Ellis was conscious of her aching, empty arms. The baby weighed almost nothing but it was like she'd been holding a bag of cement. She should embrace this woman, for what she was doing. She said, 'You were the best teacher, you know. And I'm sorry I was no good at music.'

'That doesn't matter,' she said. 'Not now.'

'By the way,' Ellis said. 'I've thought of her as Columbine. But of course you'll name her what you like.'

25

⟨ WHAT WAS IT THAT EMILY HAD BURIED, in that dream? Of all the dreams that Dove – and Ellis – had had since then, this one had not recurred. All she was left with was the sound of Emily Brontë coughing as she walked away from the lonely new grave back to her home in the parsonage, back to prepare for the remaining weeks of her life.

Dove's mother had coughed, just before she died, after Dove had finished reading her the novel and when she was first writing her story. Ellis in that story was described as being rescued from the earth. Dove had dreamed this, had witnessed the extraordinary scene where she found Ellis suffocating, in a ditch somewhere, and had dragged her out and brushed the cold soil off her clothes and warmed her back to life. She had saved her, though for what purpose she did not understand. Except now she thought back on that dream, and the scene she had written a while ago, it struck her that the landscape from which she had rescued Ellis was very similar to the moorland route that went from behind the parsonage all the way to the ruin of Top Withens and beyond, its features bare and its weather bleak. She had described it then as scrubby, and Ellis lying abandoned by a road, but it could easily have been the track across the moors where she had found her, flanked by hillocks of dry grasses and with a horizon that vanished into a green-black haze.

It struck her with a force almost as mighty as the naked wind on the Yorkshire moors that she would not discover from her dreams what it was that Emily had buried, but that it was up to her to decide, to invent it. Such secrecy, the flight across the moors before dawn, could only mean something shameful. Either that or something so intensely private, she could not dispose of it anywhere in or around her home.

It was only about seven in the morning and she was in the bathroom thinking this. Quickly she dressed and made a cup of tea and fed Viv his morning biscuits then went to her book-shelves and took out the few books about the Brontës which she thought she already knew back to front. Deciding the truth of this secret was almost heady, but while it was all her creation now, it still had to make sense. Some of the speculation about Emily was such nonsense, considering how solitary a person she was, how isolated. That she had a lover and became pregnant, or was anorexic, or had willed her own death – or all of these things – smacked of desperation, sensationalism. For Dove you would only dispose in that way one of two things: the corpse of a baby was implausible, so it could only be a book – or a manuscript.

Yes, there was some suggestion of the intensely private woman being secretly wooed, and perhaps this leading to a pregnancy which ended in miscarriage, which might explain Emily's habit of shutting herself away from everyone in the household. But this was from the lunatic fringe of Brontë fandom (she would hardly call it scholarship). More persuasive was the idea from some researchers that there had been another manuscript, which Charlotte had destroyed. That was only a theory, but to Dove it was a start. Besides, she had seen it, as clearly as everything she had seen in this dream.

She saw it again now, as she sat and made notes at her desk. She saw Emily sitting alone in her narrow bed with her writing desk on her knees, a candle in a saucer on the bedside table, a ladder-backed chair jammed under the door handle. Then she noticed that Emily was thinner, paler. She saw the title on the first page of the manuscript, the author's distinctive handwriting, smaller and tighter than her sister Charlotte's, not nearly as neat as Anne's, and retaining some childish characteristics, perhaps because of her natural left-handedness. But she knew this was not the manuscript of *Wuthering Heights*. Emily, barricaded in her room, wrote away steadily, frowning and making corrections or angrily crossing out lines here and there, and sighing as she read over the pages. Occasionally she coughed and wiped her nose, absent-mindedly using the same handkerchief to wipe her pen, which she had to mend frequently, given that she pressed so hard on the pages with it.

She always kept this manuscript locked in her desk when she was not working on it. During this time, after Branwell's funeral when she caught that cold, she became thinner, and spoke less to her family, sometimes going for days without saying a word, not even to Keeper. She rose every morning to take breakfast at her usual place at the table, ears blocked against the household around her. She fed the dogs, and performed her household tasks, and became thinner and quieter. Dove, who never heard very much at all when she peered into such scenes, nevertheless now heard the cough that accompanied her all the time, felt the horrible fluid power of it, as Emily pressed a handkerchief to her mouth. Every few days she descended to the outhouse and rinsed and wrung these handkerchiefs, pegging them out on the line that ran to the chicken coop. As the weeks went on, as the end of the year approached, they dried into small flags rigid with frost.

It was too sad. Emily was turning into an old woman, and she had not finished with being a child. She had been working hard on a manuscript that would never in her view be good enough to leave after she had gone. It was born a deformed thing, a puny weak creature that could not stand against the raw, healthy force of her firstborn. She could not have burned it in the kitchen or parlour fire for then her sister would know, and Charlotte's disapproval would be as ferocious and as unbearable as her devotion. And so that was why her only option, after reading through the entire manuscript with her brows drawn and mouth set firm against her cough, the candle guttering in the cold nights that marched even colder towards December, had been to wrap it against prying eyes, and take it as far away as she could and place it where it belonged. Dove could almost see Emily calculating: she could still walk that distance, though in a couple of weeks more she would not have the strength, and she could walk that path with her eyes closed, in her sleep if she had to, she knew it so well.

And so what perhaps was another masterpiece was consigned to the clammy earth, where every year the deep snow would pile above it and in the warmer months the worms would nibble through it like any other organic thing.

It was never Charlotte who destroyed that second novel: it could only be the author herself whose implacable courage against the inevitable was already well known. Given all that she had done, Dove knew that the other famous grim stories about Emily were nothing by comparison. Searing her arm with the hot poker after the rabid dog bite had been easy. Refusing the doctor for her consumption not worth a second thought. And dying was simply a joke.

26

⟨ ELLIS WAS ALONE IN HER OFFICE ONE
afternoon when her assistant came to the door.

'There's a woman to see you, she says she knows you.'

Over Amanda's shoulder Ellis caught sight of a familiar
figure: Mrs Wood still wore a twinset, with a small string of
pearls and a pencil skirt. She looked chic. Rising to greet her,
Ellis realised that Mrs Wood was so much older than she had
always remembered her. But of course, so was she. It must have
been at least fifteen years since they had last seen each other,
on her wedding day. Nevertheless Mrs Wood's hair was barely
touched by grey, and still in its French roll.

'Thanks Amanda. Could you get us some coffee?' She closed
the door. 'Mrs Wood. Please sit down.'

'Thank you'.

Ellis could not sit behind her desk and extend authority over this woman. She sat in one of the easy chairs under the window next to a coffee table with a stack of the latest issue of the magazine. She crossed her legs. She was wearing what she privately called her uniform: shell top with black trousers, her black jacket on a metal coat stand in a corner of the room. Sometimes she wore a jersey knit top or a silk shirt. Flat shoes and minimal jewellery.

'You never knew Frank, of course. My husband.' Mrs Wood took out a cigarette and a slim gold lighter. She now smoked Dunhill Blue. 'By the way, call me Nell. After all these years.'

'You married during the war,' Ellis said. 'I remember the photo in your sitting room, on the sideboard. You couldn't get enough material for a full wedding dress.'

'He was killed.'

'In the war.'

'Not the war you're thinking of. The Korean War.' She stubbed out her cigarette in the glazed bowl next to the magazines. 'Thirty-two Australian men were killed in the Battle of Kapyong, in April 1951.'

'I didn't know. I'm sorry.'

'No one knows, or cares. Or very few. We remember who we want, or need to. We were married seven years. Frank was a career soldier: he loved me, but he also loved what he did. Our marriage started during one war, ended in another. And what I had to show for it were a few photos. And my smoking addiction.'

'And do you still have your five o'clock G and T?'

At that Nell smiled. 'You remember? No, not any more.' She paused. 'Anyway, that's not why I've come.' She bent down to her bag and fished out a copy of *Pages* from two months previously. Ellis remembered it, though the issue had been put to bed some months before that.

'I read this article, by that activist who had the abortion in the sixties. After all these years I owe you an apology.'

Apology? Ellis had always supposed that Mrs Wood had done what she had to. Besides, she had provided a name and phone number. It was all she had needed. Ron and his fifty pounds had taken care of the rest.

The magazine had a special feature on women's sexuality and focused on myth debunking. Orgasm (vaginal or clitoral). Abortion. Sex therapy. Fantasy. Just printing words like clitoris and abortion in bold caps on the contents page had meant three meetings with the managing editor before she persuaded him. They weren't one of the other racy women's magazines, with their male centrefolds and offers of sexy makeovers for dowdy girls, magazines of endless controversy that saw editors sacked and hired nonstop and brought mentions in parliament. They were a respectable magazine for men and women alike, though their main reader was the family-minded woman, who would not expect them to sink that low. But Ellis had convinced him they needed to be topical, otherwise the circulation figures would plummet, and did they want to be relevant or not?

The issue had contained a story written by a well-known women's doctor and family planning activist about her own illegal operation, when she was a student, and the reason she had established a women's health clinic in Glebe. Even with her contacts, the medical student had been forced to seek a backyard operation, but one far worse than Ellis's experience, which had been around the same time. This woman had stayed with an aunt on the other side of the city, who had refused to talk about the operation, let alone help her. She had paid dearly for the privilege and suffered for two weeks afterwards until a kindly doctor on duty at the emergency ward of a public hospital took pity on her and scheduled her for a second procedure, to clean out the incomplete abortion and finally stop her bleeding.

'I knew what I was doing, and I sent you off to your fate.'

'Well, it could have been a lot worse,' Ellis said.

But how lucky she had been. Had she had to return for another operation, or had a D and C like the woman who'd written the story, she didn't know what she would have done. She even felt lucky that it had only cost fifty pounds, that Ron had at least escorted her until she was picked up in the back streets of Surry Hills. It had not been far from where her office was now, she realised.

'It cost me a fortune too,' Nell was saying. 'And mine was many years earlier.'

'You mean you knew exactly what it would be like?'

Nell nodded.

'And you never said?'

'No.'

'You just let me go and do it.' Ellis spoke bitterly. 'I was only seventeen.'

'So was I.'

'But you were married.'

Nell still wore her ring, a thin gold band. She gave Ellis a look.

'You mean you weren't married?'

'Of course I wasn't. And I suffered a great deal. Mostly you did. This woman's story,' she tapped the magazine, 'I could have written it.'

Ellis did not ask who the man was. She felt Nell believed she ought to know but somehow she was refusing to tell her. She waited.

Nell took another cigarette, smiling. 'Look how far you've come,' she said. 'How much you've achieved.' She looked around the office, with its long white desk, its Marimekko-print curtains framing a view of the city and harbour. It was ten floors up, and although *Pages* represented a small corner of its parent media empire, it had a strong following, with its circulation steadily increasing since Ellis had been editor. The editorial team had moved floors the year before, symbolically up a few levels into the former executive area which had been redecorated, and Ellis had acquired her own office.

'I'm still the same person.' Though Ellis knew she was not. She was nothing like the young woman who had first started as a typist and general office assistant for the cookery section of the *Women's Pages*. That person had long been buried.

And she was certainly not the girl who years before that had gone to Mrs Wood feeling faint and sick, desperately after a contact for an abortion.

'Well, yes.' Nell paused. 'Ellis, you asked me once about your mother.'

Ellis nodded.

'I wouldn't tell you anything. Do you remember her?'

Ellis did not. Tried as she had over the years, there was nothing but a blank space. Not a scrap of a lullaby or song, or the sound of a laugh, or the glimpse of a necklace, or the scent of clothing kept in a camphorwood box.

'She left when you were a baby. Your father refused to speak of her ever again.'

'I know. He still won't talk about her.'

Nell took another cigarette. 'I expect he's not mentioned the rest of his family either.'

'I didn't know there was one.'

'Have you ever gone through the photos in the tin box?'

Ellis knew what she meant. Her father kept photos and mementoes in a locked box, more of a trunk, which he rarely opened. Occasionally, when he'd had a few drinks at Christmas for instance, he'd open it and show Ellis a picture of her grandmother, or a great-uncle. People far too distant to have any meaning for her. There were a few of herself as a baby, and some of him as a small boy, solemn and rosy-cheeked, with a straw hat pushed back on his head, or sitting beside a bucket and spade on a beach, curly haired, but still frowning.

'I've wanted to,' she said, 'but somehow I can't. Not when I know he wouldn't like it.'

'Maybe you'll have to wait then,' Nell said. Ellis knew what she meant. 'One day, have a look, then we might talk again.'

'You make it sound all mysterious.' Ellis walked her out the door and down the hall to the lift.

Nell gazed at her. Her eyes were very clear, grey. Ellis realised how reserved a beauty she was. She barely had on a lick of lipstick and she was wearing the same style of clothes she'd worn most of her life, but there was a dignity, a presence about her. She could not imagine Nell being their housekeeper, the person who showed her how to remove grass stains and who had instilled in her a lifelong preference for ironed sheets.

'Well, it is mysterious. You of all people don't need me to tell you how complicated life is, how it never unfolds like a story. Goodbye, my dear.'

For the first time in her life, she pulled Ellis close and hugged her, then kissed her on the cheek and hugged her again.

27

⟮ DOVE WOULD NOT FAIL TO TELL THE
story of Charlie but the purpose of the author walking across
those dark pre-dawn moors to bury a parcel had distracted her.
By then she knew in her heart that she should not think ill of
Ellis, even though she now appeared to have abandoned a child
not once but twice. And worse. Three babies had resulted in her
being a mother to none. She should not judge, but it did seem to
her incomprehensible at best, criminal at worst. Mothers were not
meant to do this. Even Ellis's own mother leaving her as a baby
did not mean Ellis had to inherit this monstrous irresponsibility.

She resolved not to think about Ellis, to rid her from her
imagination if at all possible. In any case, perhaps the story was
all but done now. Things seemed to be explained and tidied
up. She placed the story draft onto a USB stick and wiped the

original from her laptop, then locked the stick and the printed manuscript away in a drawer of her desk, and placed the key in a wooden jewellery box kept in her wardrobe. If she was not confronted with it then maybe she could forget about it. The entire thing so filled her with despair, even faint revulsion, she shared Charlotte's view that in its own way hers was also a story of perverted passion and passionate perversity.

Of course it was not that simple. The story gnawed at her heart, when it was not burrowing through her mind. Within weeks it was pulling her back with a shocking elemental force, and she found herself unlocking the drawer and reading through her notes despite all resolve. Emily did not do this, she thought, scanning the printed manuscript and scribbling notes and corrections almost as if her hand were directed by an unseen force. Emily reserved no pity for herself and did what she needed to a defective story, when she realised she had caught consumption and would be dead within months, unable to finish it to her own ruthless satisfaction. She had found the strength of will to let it go entirely. But Dove could not. Just as before, when she had tried to distract herself, nothing worked. She was as bound to the story as ever.

By now she had lost all pretence in living a normal life. She couldn't remember the last time she had been out, or even if she had any existence of consequence left, after these past few months. If it were not for the cat she might go entire days without speaking, and even then Viv's conversational demands were minimal. Were she to sit any longer in that cold damp house she might develop mould as if she were just another leather boot or furnishing, the ottoman, or her writing table.

It was at times like this that she felt acutely the lack of any family. If she had her mother, or a sister, or a brother, she could pick the phone up and whinge and be herself, which is what families were for, and not feel guilty for neglecting them. It was different with friends, unless they were very close, and in the last few years the only person she could call close was Martin. But Passageway had been so busy lately that going there for a drink was no guarantee of having a chat.

It was a cloudy afternoon. The rain had been drizzling on and off for a week, and that was the excuse she had given herself for lying low, and again the reason she returned to her manuscript despite her earlier resolve. She would go for a walk. She pushed her chair back from her desk, not realising the cat was so close. He leaped to one side and mewed with alarm. She inspected the sky from the damp and dripping back verandah. It looked like there was a hint of sun. After tucking a folding umbrella into the pocket of her coat she set off. As soon as she slammed the front door Viv leaped to the table at the window and stared at her through the wooden venetians, his eyes narrowed to kalamata olives. She turned away. Perhaps she should get a dog, which would mean she would have to walk, get out every day.

The air was crisp, despite the damp. As if to punish herself Dove walked straight towards Parramatta Road, then turned left, heading west. The rush of the traffic and the need to stay alert crossing side streets and negotiating pedestrian lights would keep her occupied enough until eventually she became bored, tramping along like some dogged backpacker in hope of something rewarding, a view or a monument. She had never walked this way along Parramatta Road, and it was clearly not designed for pedestrians. Of course: who would even consider walking along such a thoroughfare, choosing it for a place to stroll for pleasure? She passed block after block of sad businesses, many of them vacant shops, some furniture places, vast and empty of customers; a discount clothing store, a café that seemed stuck in 1958, a steakhouse, a bicycle repair shop. She was approaching the rise that peaked with Fort Street school to her left before she realised that she had passed Annandale and not given a thought to her story. At the top of the hill she looked down to the road that dipped under the railway bridge. Farther on there were more vast commercial blocks, the garden art place a foretaste of the discount furniture and baby accessory stores which would be followed by kilometres filled with hotels and car yards and building suppliers and barely a soul to be seen except in a car.

As she continued walking, it came rushing back. The whole first scene, the starting chapter, that was at first just a story of its own but was now like a quarry that she returned to again and again, mining for narrative. When she began writing the story, Ellis was on the bus visiting her father. Dove stopped and looked back. She had just passed a bus stop, so she decided to walk back to it and wait. It was midafternoon, a weekday, and buses thundered past her on each side of the roadway. They would be getting more and more frequent as peak hour approached. Where would Ellis have caught her bus? She lived farther down Annandale, about halfway between here and the bay, so would have walked all the way up to Parramatta Road, perhaps getting the bus somewhere near Johnston Street. It seemed natural that Dove would sit at the bus stop and wait. It was silly, but as a bus passed her she scanned the inside looking for a young woman with a baby on her lap. In a few minutes another bus paused. It was a 483, to Strathfield via Ashfield. She alighted and fished her Opal card out of her purse, waving it over the machine as the bus door whirred shut with pneumatic ease.

Dove sat about halfway along, on the left, at a window seat. It was all so possible. Here she was being carried towards Ashfield and it was as if it was meant to be. There were few people on the bus and it whizzed along for despite the increasing flow of traffic there were infrequent stops this far west of the city, unlike the ones Dove was accustomed to, and the bus had its own lane painted brick red. Was Ellis's bus also a 483? Dove had not considered that at the time. It was a green and cream single decker bus with windows that only opened if you pushed them hard. Hers was sealed shut, clean and airconditioned, even on a mild day. The fabric seats were covered in a bold anti-graffiti pattern, and there were two sets of red seats facing each other, to be vacated for the elderly or the disabled. Sometimes these seats were occupied by people with the enormous prams that were everywhere these days, massive but smooth-functioning things which parents, mainly mothers, pushed directly up ramps and parked into place. Back in 1968 Ellis had had to take Charlie out of his stroller, fold it down, then stand and carry him balanced on one arm, the stroller on the other along with her shoulder bag, while she struggled onto the hot, ill-ventilated bus which lurched as it pulled away and lurched again when it stopped. The passengers were so thrust and jerked about it was if the driver held a grudge. Holding onto a baby in these circumstances was hard work. Then when Ellis alighted at the stop in Liverpool Road, she had to do the same thing in reverse, with no one to help her, and then at the gate to her father's house she had got Charlie out of the stroller again.

Charlie. Dove would work it out, she would.

The bus turned into Liverpool Road and she realised she would be getting off soon. Even though she had never really decided what street Ellis had lived in as a child, she knew it must be somewhere around Victoria Street, for she could see the Canary Island date palms, massive even back then. And despite the fact that many of these places were ruined or compromised by unsympathetic renovations, or turned into boarding houses, or destroyed entirely and the blocks turned into flats, she could see enough to know she was getting close.

She alighted at the stop after the 7-Eleven. From here on the streetscape changed dramatically. It would be barely recognisable to the Ellis who had lived here until the 1960s. It was a crammed stretch – noodle houses, travel agents, Korean BBQ restaurants, moneylenders, pide shops – with the civic centre and shopping mall planted firmly in the middle. The tiny plaza was forever busy, if not with shoppers and pub-goers, then with the incorrigible pigeons, or ibis that colonised the palm canopies and lorikeets that raided them in screaming twilight posses. It was not a restful place.

As she turned to walk back she found she was right outside the School of Arts, squashed between a Turkish pide house and an unremarkable office building. It had the original lettering above the door, *SCHOOL OF ARTS 1912*, and in every respect looked unchanged since Ellis was a girl. It now seemed to be home to several small businesses. Peering through the frosted glass doors, Dove strained to see a glimpse of the interior, but quickly backed off down the steps in case anyone thought she was prying. Inside and to the left had been the meeting room where Ellis had learned ballet for a short time until it had become apparent that she had no real talent for it. The teacher had had a quiet word with Nell Wood, who brought Ellis along to lessons once a week when she was six or seven, and encouraged more practice at home during the term breaks. She had loaned them some short-playing records for the purpose, an extract from Handel's *Water Music*, the drill-like first few minutes of 'Boléro', to stimulate flow and encourage precision, respectively. In the front room Mrs Wood would push back the furniture and roll up the rug while Ellis swayed and bent emulating a willow tree in the breeze, or marched with her limbs as straight as possible. After performing in the annual Christmas pageant, where Ellis to her humiliation was cast in the role of a boy, she refused to re-enrol, and it was a relief to everyone.

Dove passed the police station and crossed the road to a small park. Straight ahead, she thought, was the way, but she turned into the park first. It was carpeted with couch grass, distinctively blue-green, in need of mowing. Its garden beds contained camellias and azaleas, some still in bloom, and there were large eucalyptus nicholii flanking either side, which must have been planted some twenty or thirty years ago. After the rain, their pepperminty smell lingered in the air. She crossed the park and came out to another street, which all of a sudden became quiet, though it was only metres from Victoria Road, and was wide and shady. Some of the houses were enormous and looked like they had remained untouched for decades. Farther down she saw the street name – Tintern – and then passed another huge house named Arundel. Romantic names, steeped in legend. It was tempting to find Ellis's family home here, but as beautiful as the prospect was, Dove knew this was not it.

Victoria Square was a grassy block of tall trees down the centre of the road, like a private green lung for the residents, untouched, not landscaped, barely tidied. Summer nights, she guessed, they would gather for barbecues or, on weekends, for kids' parties. She could easily imagine fairy lights strung through the trees, and tea candles in jars placed on sawn-off logs or other makeshift picnic tables, while people shared platters of hummus and Turkish bread and dug canned drinks out of plastic tubs filled with ice.

Children could run around all day in this place and be totally safe, it was that quiet. She walked all the way around Victoria

Square, wondering if this was where Charlie had played when he was little, or his mother, but developing the distinct sense that he did not. The street she knew without doubt was the one where Ellis had lived was back around the corner, but as she turned into it and approached the next roundabout she knew with increasing certainty that Charlie had not.

On the opposite side of the road a private hospital sprawled across one entire block. Each side of the road featured squat red brick flats that had replaced Federation houses, built in the 1960s or later. When Ellis walked home from the bus stop she would have passed them as building sites. Maybe men on scaffolding had whistled to her as she walked with her head erect trying to ignore them. Or maybe they had all been built in a sudden spurt of development in the four years she was away at high school. On the next corner a man was on a ladder painting the side eaves of a house that stretched back way out of her sight but featured five chimneys. A miniature version of the house sat beside it, possibly once the garage, or servants' quarters. He paused and stared at her as she passed, pushing back a conical coolie hat. Then he took out a handkerchief from the front pocket of his overalls and rubbed it across his face before dipping a long thin paintbrush into a small tin and applying it with slow meticulous strokes.

To her left was a row of houses with sentinel Canary Island date palms, the same concrete footpath that had been here for decades, and the whiff of domestic activity faint but unmistakable, though now it contained the scent of spices – star anise and pepper, she thought – rather than onions and boiled meat.

And here was the first part of the story of Ellis unfolding as if it had all been true, as if the house she now faced had indeed been the family home to people she had only invented. Except for the fact that a clipped murraya hedge replaced the plumbago, and the green wire gate was now a smart picket one painted in pale grey, this was the house where Ellis's father had opened the door that morning and said 'Hi-de-hi!' as his grandson took his very first wobbly steps on the path leading to the front verandah.

Dove placed her hand on the picket gate then removed it. Something was wrong. She could see the scene that had replayed in her mind a thousand times, the scene so vivid where her story had first begun. It was as if it had happened just this morning, but there was a piece missing. And it was not like the last section of a jigsaw puzzle either, it was the entire scene, as complete as it could be but lacking one vital element. On that day in her story her first glimpse of Ellis had been when she was alone on the bus. Dove had then gone back and viewed the scene again, and then rewritten it to comment on the fact that she could not say at what point she'd realised Ellis had a baby.

It was a relief, when she finally understood it, even though it upset her as well. She could not say because it had not happened. She could not finish the story of Charlie because he had never existed. Standing there at the gate, her eyes suddenly stupid with tears, Dove knew she had invented him, and she had done it because she needed him. She needed him more than Ellis.

28

⁌ THE TIN WAS A BIT LARGER THAN A lunch box. It looked like its original purpose had been as a strongbox or cash tin, Ellis never knew. It had just always been there, always fastened shut, painted a green so dark it was nearly black. Only now and then did she remember her father opening it. She took it down from the top shelf of the cupboard in the spare room and placed it on the bed. She sat beside it for a moment, then realising how dusty the box was, took it out to the kitchen bench and wiped it clean. Light poured into her apartment through the French doors. The place was only small but positioned to capture the sun. A few years back, after she had settled all her father's affairs, she had moved from the Potts Point flat and bought a place of her own nearby. Recently she had done it out in unforgiving white and pale grey.

Then she sat down in front of the coffee table and opened the tin. There was no lock now but the clasp had rusted with age. After she flicked it back she needed to fetch a knife to prise the tin box open. She took a breath. The sweetish musty smell of old paper. How long since it had been opened, she had no idea. All her father's papers, his chequebook, his will, his long expired passport, the deeds to the house, had been kept in an expanding manila file in the left-hand compartment of his wardrobe, for as long as she could remember. After his death she had known to go straight there and hand over everything the solicitor needed for probate. It was in exactly the place it was meant to be. It was almost as if her father were still there, having asked her to fetch the file for him so he could write a cheque. Banking had instilled a sense of disciplined ceremony in Edgar when it came to the household finances. When it was time to settle accounts, he would sit at the kitchen table with a tidy sheaf of bills, unscrew a fountain pen kept specially for the purpose, and write three or four cheques, blotting each with an old-fashioned wooden ink blotter that he would roll from side to side. Ellis, when she was very young, would be allowed to help tuck the cheques into envelopes, which he then addressed and blotted and handed to her so she could lick the stamps. When she was a little older, she was allowed to walk up to the postbox on her own.

After the funeral director had been paid and the household bills finalised, she returned the chequebook to the bank herself and closed his two accounts. She supposed she could have done all that by mail or over the phone, but she had always liked visiting the branch in Liverpool Road where he had worked for most of his life.

When she sold the house she sent his clothes off to the Smith Family and organised a dealer to come and give her a quote for the furniture. The rest she sorted through as quickly as possible, taking very little. The ornaments had never interested her, the few vases were impractical. There had never been any formal family portraits, just the one photo of her wedding which she took out of its cheap frame and tucked into the dark blue photo album that she had started when she was a schoolgirl, with her Box Brownie. Going through all the utensils, the crockery, the garden tools, she saw that there was nothing she wanted to keep. She threw out the contents of the cupboards and left the cleaning things in the laundry for the contract people who came when the house was empty, before the new owners moved in.

That was almost three years ago and since then the tin box had gone straight into the spare room. She did not know why she could never bring herself to open it. The desire to know about her mother was something that had flooded through her almost from nowhere when she was a girl, when she went to boarding school, when she was sixteen. She had felt it like an unstoppable force of nature, like rain swelling then breaching a dam, rising and rising to flood through her entire being. If she did not do something about it she might drown. But Nell Wood had refused to discuss it and she had had to swallow down the tide. Then over the years it had lapped at her periodically – on her wedding day when she turned around to walk back down the aisle; on the day she left Vince; after her baby was born and she took her away on the train – until Nell came visiting her at her office that day.

Her father was frail by then, but he had regular visits from community nurses and the local volunteer organisations and there had never been any discussion about moving to somewhere smaller. He had made some practical changes to accommodate his arthritis so that he did not need to use most of the house, remaining in the front rooms where he could shuffle on his frame from the television and to the bathroom and back to his bed across the hall. With meals delivered every weekday, the cleaner on Fridays, a man for the gardens every other weekend, scarcely a day went by when someone didn't visit. He agreed to keep the cordless phone always nearby and Ellis rang every afternoon and visited on the weekends, taking cakes and other treats, though his appetite had shrunk. Everything about her father had shrunk. When he found it too exhausting to go out for Sunday lunch, something they had done for years, she realised it would not be too long.

In those final years only once more had she asked about her mother and he had set his mouth and pretended not to hear.

'Dad,' she had said again, looking directly at him. He had tried to get out of his chair but had sat back again, gesturing to the television.

'Turn it up please.'

Ellis had pressed the button. She decided she would have to get him a remote control, to make it easier.

She always suspected there were things in the tin box that would reveal the truth about her mother. She knew where it was kept and could have fetched it herself and had a quiet look. Indeed she could have taken it away and kept it and he would never have known, except she could not do that. It remained in its place in the sideboard cupboard, the cupboard that would have contained cork-backed placemats and the collection of wax fruit, except she had thrown all those things out years back.

The memories of all those old things. The house and its contents, for years so dark and dreary, was, until she was sixteen or seventeen, the only kind of home she had known existed. And all that her father had known too, apparently. It had never struck her, until now, reaching into the box and its cool musty contents, that when she redecorated that front room, moving out the dark brown carpet and covering the lounge seats with plain light fabric, how much that must have disturbed him. Her father had agreed to it but not approved. Now she understood that the place must have been exactly as it had been when her mother disappeared, when she was just a baby, and that he needed that house to remain like a wax bouquet under a glass dome.

The first photo was of a woman seated in that same room, taken decades ago but the room, uncannily, appeared just as it was when she had lived there as a girl. It was like a still from a black and white film of her childhood. There was the same oak planter she remembered, but containing a madonna lily. Beside it the woman was seated on a ladder-backed chair, her body partially turned to her left where there was a small round table containing the tea service. She faced the camera, but her features were fuzzy. It was as if she were about to pour tea and someone had persuaded her to pause for the camera. She was not smiling. The curtains behind her had been pushed aside, causing the light coming through the window to obscure half her face. Ellis had removed those velvet curtains and the ecru lace ones behind them. They always smelled of dust. There was a wooden window seat, one of her favourite places to sit when she was a child, watching out for the baker or the postman.

She sat back in her chair. Now she remembered Nell Wood's polishing of the same silver tea service that was never used, the weekly dusting ritual of the dining room, which they used on Christmas Day and never any other time. The ugly dried flower arrangements that Nell had done her best with, taking them outside and shaking them upside down to shift the dust, before spraying them with VO5 to hold the delicate petals and feathery stems in place, to make them last as long as possible. In her cleaning and redecorating frenzy Ellis had taken them and tossed them into the bin one afternoon while her father was at bowls. When he came home and saw the bare mantelpiece that she was painting with undercoat he turned on his heel at the door and went to his sitting room with the Sunday paper.

Holding the contents of the box, she let the reel of memories scroll across her mind, and it was just like she was watching a film, albeit a surreal one full of odd leaps and vacant chunks of the narrative. She saw herself sitting hunched on her bed all that awful afternoon, before striding down the backyard to burn the photographs, then returning to start cleaning the kitchen. She remembered how dinner was late that day since she had lost track of time. She had cooked potatoes, new ones, in their jackets, and fried sausages with onion gravy, which she hated but her father loved. She had emptied the vegetable bin and taken it outside and scrubbed it. And after dinner and all the next day she had continued cleaning, getting down on the floor again to scrub the lino upon which years and years of floor polish had yellowed the pale green and pink rose pattern like a thick layer of varnish. As she scrubbed she saw Mrs Wood mopping with a cotton cloth tied with string to an old flat broom, which gave a better result, she said, than a usual mop. Before Mrs Wood, who would have cleaned this floor? Her mother maybe, and her grandmother certainly. Perhaps before that a maid or the weekly help. The idea of all these women on their knees like her scrubbing away grime then layering on floor polish, only to have to strip it off again with yet more scrubbing, filled her with a sense of outrage. She determined she would have the lino taken out as soon as she could and replaced with something more practical. In one corner where it wouldn't show she turned back a section to discover layers of newspaper stained the colour of tea. Under that were floorboards, oiled and black with age.

In the event, she had not, but instead had turned her energies to the front room, which she had transformed, ensuring that whatever she did she would make it as different to the way it had always been, for as long as she remembered. But after all that she had not used that room very much. She had sat there and played records and painted her nails on weekends, or tackled her various craft projects at nights after work. Not so long afterwards she had married Vince and moved out. In her head she could hear a single forever playing 'Eleanor Rigby' on her white portable record player, while seeing herself seated beside the front window making macramé placemats from burnt orange string.

All the photos in the tin box were grainy. There were no more of the woman in the first photo seated in the front room. Her dress suggested it was taken in the 1920s, and although her hair was piled on her head she looked to be quite young. Perhaps it was her grandmother. The next photos were group shots of people she did not know. She recognised the front verandah of the house, and the back garden. There was one of three young men standing on the lawn in cricket whites. Inspecting one closer, she was sure the middle man was her father, his hair clipped close at the sides and brushed to one side of his forehead, rather than combed straight back as he had always worn it. Another photo showed two boys, no more than eight or ten, again seated in the front room, this time in the matching ladder-backed chairs that she had removed to the dining room. Here again was surely her father, who was slightly older, and beside him a much darker version but some of the features were similar. Her father had had dirty blond hair and fair skin, and he was always returning from bowls with a burnt nose despite his hat. It was definitely him, with the solemn mouth that rose slightly higher at one side than the other. The boy next to him had the same shaped eyebrows and full-lipped mouth, though his smile seemed forced. But his brows were dark and somehow he was frowning at the same time he had produced a sneering sort of smile for the photographer. He was seated on the edge of the chair and everything about his attitude suggested he did not want to be there.

She had no idea her father had had a brother, but then she had no idea about any of the family. The final photograph was in a cream envelope, discoloured and foxed with age. She held it up to her nose before slipping her fingers inside. There was a faint smell, stale and floral. She was sure it was the scent of violets. She drew out a photo of herself with her father. Except it was not she, not unless she was clad in a formal wedding dress. And she had never worn her hair as long as that. Nor was she as petite as this woman. But her own eyes, however – striking, dark – stared back, the face directed straight at the camera with a bold, almost ironic, smile. Beside the woman her father seemed a good deal older. And it was the only photograph of him where he was smiling, indeed his face was half turned to the woman beside him as if he had never seen anything more beautiful in his life. In the second or two it took her to realise the truth she dropped all the contents of the tin box onto the table.

29

⟪ THE GRANGE WAS IN STRATHFIELD. SHE took the bus and train, then walked up from the main shopping centre to Redmyre Road. The streets here always reminded her of Ashfield, except they were even wider, and the properties – at least the ones that hadn't been subdivided – were enormous. The houses were mostly flanked by trees, and shrubs protected the front gardens from the street beyond. The Grange was like many of the houses, set back from the road with a curving driveway. This was spread with white gravel which crunched agreeably as she walked along it. At the entrance only the stainless steel handrails and security cameras betrayed the fact it was a nursing home. Ellis supposed out of all the aged residential care facilities, if that was their correct term, this would have to be one of the nicer. Once a vast house, it still maintained the appearance of a family home. The sign out the front could have been for a wedding reception place or a particularly exclusive club. The receptionist opened the door when she buzzed. On her desk was an oil burner lit by a tea candle and the air was suffused with the scent of lemon verbena. Aside from the introduction of the oil burner, nothing had ever changed since Ellis had first started visiting.

Nell Wood was expecting her. She welcomed her in to a small but airy sitting room.

'Why don't we sit here?' She gestured to a spot next to the casement window that opened on to the side of the house near the back. The gravel drive stretched past the window, and beyond it was a narrow bed of azaleas against the fence. Tradesmen and delivery vans used the driveway on the other side of the house that ran around to the rear of the property, but here, aside from the gardener or the occasional patient, it was quiet and private. The Grange suited Nell Wood's cloistered life, which had always been conducted as an adjunct to others. Moving from her flat, when the stairs became too much, to this small residence had not proved difficult for her pragmatic nature.

Nell set out cups and Ellis drew out the packet of almond biscuits – the older woman's favourites – she had bought at the delicatessen on the way. Then she reached into her bag again and pulled out the tin box. Nell took the biscuits into her kitchenette and returned with them on a plate, and the coffee pot. The box seemed very large and dark there on the tea table.

'So you finally opened it?'

Ellis nodded. 'You knew what was inside?'

'Vaguely. I've never looked myself. Only photos?'

'Yes.' Ellis opened the box and pulled out the photos, turning them over one at a time until she reached the final one. Nell regarded each of them without changing her expression, until the final one was placed before her. She took it up and stared at it for a long time, then placed it down and looked at Ellis.

'They were married, then? But when did she leave? And why?'

Nell Wood sighed and gazed out the window for a long time before turning to face Ellis again. Her eyes were still clear and bright, unfaded by age.

'Her name was Catherine.' She paused, looking around and gesturing as if still after the cigarettes she had finally given up, before settling back in her seat and holding her hands together. 'And I do wish your father had told you all this,' she said.

'But you knew he never would. I need to know what happened.'

Nell Wood poured the coffee and handed Ellis her cup.

'You were just a baby. So he contacted me. I moved to that flat closer to your house, and came around every day, sometimes from early morning. I continued to look after you and the house until you went off to high school.'

'I remember all that,' Ellis said. But she knew she didn't. She only remembered Mrs Wood from later in her childhood, when she was five or six, fetching her from primary school and taking her home to mind her while she prepared the evening meal. She took her shopping, and for a while to ballet lessons once a week, and sometimes she helped Ellis with school projects, or got her into the bath early, but mostly as soon as Edgar walked in the door from work, she put on her hat and coat and picked up her bag and left.

'Did you know him, before?'

'Yes, we did. Frank and I. We were all friends, as it happened. When we were younger.'

'All?'

'Your father and your mother, my husband and I.'

Nell Wood had never been anything but kind. She had helped her out when she was in the greatest need. But she was not warm, not *kindly*, Ellis realised. She could be telling her so much more. She could have told her things years ago. Ellis longed to ask but the woman seemed to have an effect on her, making her tongue remain trapped. She persisted.

'Why did she leave?'

Nell shrugged. 'She was unhappy. Very unhappy. Only the unhappiest of women leave their beautiful babies.'

Ellis's chest heaved. She was not prone to lung problems but every time she was distressed her chest felt like it was being crushed. She breathed in deeply.

'You need to tell me everything!' She had not meant to speak so loudly.

'Everything?' Nell raised her eyebrows. 'Whose story is this? Have you never asked yourself that?'

'What do you mean?'

'I mean, have you not considered that there are other people who have suffered?'

Ellis realised she was referring to herself. Nell Wood had moved to her flat to be closer to Ellis and her father, which must have been a great step for her. And they had all been friends when they were young, the four of them. The meagre facts were studded in her mind against a greater more persistent image that formed the background to her childhood: Mrs Wood departing as soon as her father arrived home. They were never in the house together for more than a few minutes.

*

WHAT, DOVE WONDERED, had she done? Or had she done it? Maybe it had happened exactly like this and she was merely recording the facts. The two women seated in Nell Wood's small flat in the nursing home were both staring out the window, saying very little. She wanted them to keep speaking, she wanted to hear Nell Wood tell her story and explain to Ellis all that she knew, and yet here was Nell herself providing a glimpse into her own past, and indicating the story was not nearly so simple as she – and Ellis – had assumed.

Nell Wood was the only person who could provide a key to Ellis's past and it was clearly Dove who had placed her there, once more visualising the journey she took, involving a bus from Potts Point and then a train, and the walk along the strip of shops from Strathfield station up to and then along Redmyre Road. Through Ellis she had seen the pleasant properties, their gardens lush with rhododendrons and cabbage tree palms. She had noted that already many of them had been subdivided, and understood that some of the beautiful old homes had been destroyed to build home units and what were now popularly being called villas, a developer's term to impart a bucolic mystique to places that in reality crammed ten or more dwellings into blocks that formerly only held one. But yet again all that she could see was merely a small part of the picture. She sensed that a great deal was happening out of her line of sight and that no matter how hard she twisted her head there would always be things running across a screen well past the corner of her eye.

At what point she had begun thinking of these characters as women and not characters she could not say. All she knew was that they had so effectively developed into real creations, ones whose waking moments were punctuated by the same pain and frustration as hers, and whose dreams were as potent as any she had ever experienced, that their inability to discuss what she felt they should be discussing was almost too much for her to bear. The thick glass wall to which she was now accustomed when viewing these characters was firmly in place, so she was not surprised that yet again she could not hear a thing. She saw them sitting there drinking their coffee in an infuriatingly reserved manner, refusing to speak, and no matter how much she pummelled on the glass or shouted, they were oblivious to her presence.

She could have cried with the frustration and with the shocking burden of all that she understood, details of both their pasts she had never known before. Here they were, now leaning forward to pick up the photographs again, then Ellis replacing them in the tin box. Then Nell was walking into her kitchenette while Ellis went to the bathroom. The bathroom was beige. Dove noted its distinct institutional décor, undisguised despite Nell Wood's efforts to personalise it with a raindrop-patterned shower curtain and thick dusty-pink towels. Ellis patted her hands on the guest towel and replenished her lipstick in the mirror. She wore a red shade which contrasted strikingly with her dark blue eyes. She was capping the lipstick and putting it back in her shoulder bag. She was going to leave soon and still they had not said all they needed to say. If Dove could have hammered on the bathroom door and hauled Ellis out and sat her down again and instructed her to stay while fetching Nell Wood back from the kitchenette, she surely would have done so. But there Nell was, coolly rinsing the cups, then tipping the coffee grounds into a small plastic bucket under the sink. She could have taken her by the shoulders – and shaken her, really, she was that incensed with the composure of this woman – and made her face Ellis and said to her, 'Look at her, look at the pain this woman has undergone all her life, and all she wants is the truth.' There was so much to be said.

Then it struck Dove how much Nell Wood's reticence masked her own suffering. As frustrated as she was, she began to see that both these women were full of memories swollen with pain, and for Nell in particular they were ones that had been contained for so long that speaking was a near impossibility.

The tragedy of an entire family threatened never to be revealed, let alone resolved, and once more in the writing of this narrative she was powerless to fix it.

3 0

⸿ THE REGISTRY OF BIRTHS, DEATHS AND Marriages was tucked in behind Railway Square. As soon as she crossed Quay Street she could smell the brew of scents emanating from Chinatown. It was a mix familiar yet hard to identify. Star anise seemed to be at the centre of it. Just after opening time, there were no other customers about. She took a blank form from the clerk at the counter and sat down to fill it out. It required her full present name, her full former name, and her place and date of birth. She could only guess at the place. She wrote a question mark in square brackets and the date, then underneath her mother's first name and her father's full name: Edgar Ernest Shaw. By the time she dated and signed the form and took it back, the clerk had a queue of several people. Ellis waited in line, then pushed the paper over. The clerk frowned.

'There are blanks here.'

'Yes, I know. But I don't have that information.'

'You don't know your mother's full name, before her marriage? Or where you were born?'

Ellis did not even know when her mother and father were married. There had been no certificate in the tin box. And he had certainly not kept a copy in the old cardboard expanding file.

The clerk blew out of her mouth. 'This might be tricky,' she said. 'And you've signed it here without a witness.'

She hadn't realised it was meant to be signed in the presence of a witness.

'Could I submit it anyway and see what happens? And maybe you could witness it. Please?'

The clerk shook her head again. 'Sorry, you'll have to do it again, then bring it to me to be signed in my presence. Anyone could be applying for this, you know.'

'No, I didn't. But how likely is that?' Ellis could not imagine why another person would be wanting her birth certificate, why anyone would be interested enough in her life.

Then the clerk proceeded to tell her a long elaborate tale about how many fake passports were being obtained. People were applying for birth certificates of the deceased, people who had died very young, and who would have been of similar age. Furnished with these, they could then go to the Passports Office and get as many passports as they wanted. This way drug dealers and other criminals were evading detection, dealing and committing other crimes all around the world. Even babies' identities were being appropriated in this way. How disgraceful was that.

'How do they get the details of dead people?' Ellis said. The clerk regarded her as if she were stupid.

'They just go to the cemeteries,' she said. 'Walk around until they spot a suitable grave, note down the full name, and the parents, and come in here. That's why we're required to enforce regulations strictly,' she concluded.

All those people roaming graveyards and cemeteries with such a pragmatic and criminal purpose. The prospect struck Ellis as somewhat fanciful, but then she had never been one to visit cemeteries. She had not done so even once, her entire life, until after her father died. She had known people who had died, that was true, but when she was younger her father had not taken her to funerals since he didn't believe that children should be exposed to them. And when she was older only people distant to her had died. It had never occurred to her to visit a cemetery but now the idea took shape: perhaps if she visited the local cemeteries she might find more clues about her mother.

But in the meantime, how having her signature witnessed in the presence of someone she had never met until half an hour ago could confirm her identity and assist national security was beyond Ellis's understanding. Still, it would not do to question the clerk. She would not wish to jeopardise her search even more. She took another blank form and filled it out again, this time leaving the space for a signature and writing Ashfield in her place of birth. It was her best guess. She queued again, waiting even longer, and took it back to the clerk. The woman solemnly scrutinised Ellis's hand as she signed her name, then took the form, turned it around, held it up and slowly read across every line, her mouth a tight purse of concentration. When she was done she placed it on the counter and in a slow childish hand wrote her name above 'Signature of Witness', then the address of the registry. She took an enormous stamp and pressed it hard on the bottom right-hand corner of the form.

'That will be forty dollars, please.'

*

FOUR WEEKS LATER A manila envelope poked out of the letterbox slot in the foyer of her block of flats. When she pulled it out a fistful of flyers for local shops fell out onto the floor. Ellis realised the floor was becoming littered with them, and not just from her slot. She put her umbrella and bag down on the terrazzo floor and gathered them up into a pile. The floor needed a good sweep too. Leaves had gathered in the corners and she could only imagine the dust. She didn't know why the building manager did not do his job better and organise more regular cleaning. She hated the way the elegant little Art Deco block of flats, just eight of them, was beginning to look so down at heel. At least when she got upstairs, to her top-floor flat, she was in her own world, with her modern kitchen and pale timber floors, and views of the city both day and night.

The automatic light, activated by pushing hard on a large plastic button that slowly eased back out, went off while she was on her knees. She had been later than usual leaving work, and the foyer was gloomy due to the rain. She got up and pushed the button back in, quickly collected the junk mail and went out the doors and down the side to the garbage bins, not bothering with her umbrella. Inside her flat she dumped her bag on the kitchen bench and fetched the broom and dustpan from the hall cupboard, then went back downstairs, propping the foyer door open with a wooden chock before sweeping the floor. The downstairs neighbour walked in, straight over the pile of dirt. He apologised, shaking his umbrella out and leaving a puddle under the letterbox slots. He apologised again but it was as if he was unaware how it got there.

By the time she fetched her mop and dried the floor and washed her hands and poured a glass of white wine she had almost forgotten about the envelope. It was sticking out the top of her bag in the bench. She decided to watch the ABC news first.

*

SHE HAD A TOASTED CHEESE sandwich for dinner sitting at the kitchen bench with another glass of wine. The television was still on. After eating she rubbed a damp finger over her plate, collecting all the crumbs and sucking her finger. When the last crumb was cleaned she pushed her plate aside and took out the envelope. It was a simple business letter size, with the return address of the Registry of Births, Deaths and Marriages stamped in small black lettering in the top left-hand corner. She peered closer at the address. It was printed in an official typeface, one of the forbidding black-letter styles favoured by the government printer. She sighed and slipped her finger along the seal.

Somehow she thought the document inside would look old too, with compressed type and numerous stamps and flourishes. But it was relatively simple, with the bluish stamp of the Principal Registrar next to a printed signature, initialled in red biro. It was pink, with faint diagonal white stripes. Baby girl pink.

She placed the document on the bench and smoothed it out, exhaling. She realised she had been holding her breath. Her name was simply her first name, she had no middle one, and under that was the date. These were the only certain facts she had ever known. The remainder was new. Under *Parents* her father was listed first but it was not her father's correct name. It said: *Clifford Shaw. Occupation Landlord, Aged 30 years, Birthplace Haberfield, NSW.* Her mother was listed, *Christian name* and *Maiden surname*, as *Catherine Ellis Granger, Aged 22 years, Birthplace Tasmania.* In the box next to *Informant* was the name *Edgar E. Shaw* and their address in Ashfield. Against

Witnesses to the birth were the names *Doctor Hare* and *Sister M. Bede.*

As the tears pooled the sudden crazy ideas running through her head receded and the story began to become clear. There had not been a silly typographical error at registration. It was not a mistake that her father's first name was entered as Clifford, or his occupation landlord instead of bank manager. The name Catherine Ellis Granger loomed out from the page, then receded. She had all the information she wanted, but still nothing was clear.

31

———

❡ I TOLD YOU YOUR MOTHER LEFT WHEN you were a baby, said Nell Wood on Ellis's final visit. And that was true but there was more to it than that. In the first instance it was not your mother who went away, but your father, for a brief period. After he returned, I came to look after you and maintain as much of a household as I could for both of you, until you were old enough.

There were a lot of mysterious goings-away in that family. Edgar and his brother had long left the family home, Edgar to study accountancy, and then to pursue a traineeship with a branch of the bank in a small town out west. Cowra, I think it was. And Cliff went away to sea at first, the merchant navy. He was always restless. He returned and left several times before he was in his twenties. When your grandmother became ill and bedridden Cliff was away, no one seemed to know where, and he could not be contacted. Edgar was assistant manager at the local branch by then. He sorted out the arrangements so that she could be looked after at home, while he kept working. He moved her into the larger front room and gave up his own room for the district nurses, who came every day, and moved into the smaller one at the back, your bedroom later on. She remained like that for several years, until the last few weeks when they took her to a ward at Concord hospital. The house was left unchanged apart from his mother's personal belongings, which he took away. After that he lived there alone, until he married Catherine.

Looking after his mother all those years had used up all his youth, though he also looked a good deal older than he was. So when he met her, your mother, it was like entering another world. They met one night at a dance in the old Eureka dance hall in Surry Hills, not far from Central Station. It later became a garment factory I think. Some friend of Edgar had dragged him along, because I gather dances and such were not really his thing.

He loved her from the moment he met her. He asked her to dance every number for the rest of the night. This was just after the war. Men were returning and young people like us were dancing everywhere, including Frank, who had joined the army when he was fifteen, right after leaving school. It was always his dream. Edgar had wanted to join up right from the start, but he couldn't leave his mother. Cliff had disappeared again and Edgar resented it, I know. He doubted Cliff had joined up to fight, though I still wonder: a war would have suited Cliff's reckless spirit. Like everything, he would have turned his experiences in a war into one big adventure.

Catherine was from Brisbane, or so she said. Right from the start I wasn't inclined to believe her, since she seemed so vague, so evasive, but I suppressed my instinctive suspicions. It sounds irrational, but to me she looked like she was from a much colder climate than Brisbane. There was something in the way she wore her gloves and threw on her fake fur cape that suggested she was used to dressing for the cold.

Frank adored dancing. He took me out every opportunity he could, dancing swing numbers. He was a wonderful dancer, fast and elegant. I could never match him, barely keep up with him. We went to the Eureka every Saturday night for as long as I can remember. This night, Edgar bumped into me coming back from the punchbowl in the side room. He spilled pink drink all over my white lawn blouse. Frank came over to see what the fuss was about, and they shook hands while I held the punch cups, then Edgar explained why he was so excited and clumsy.

'I've just met the most enchanting creature,' he said, nodding over to where Catherine sat on a stool at a table. I thought she had a dangerous beauty. Her dark hair and distinctive eyes struck me as almost gothic. Her skin was always very pale.

She was still wearing her hat and gloves, which were kid, fine and soft grey, when all the other women had discarded theirs for the night. Beside her I felt shabby, and there was that stain where Edgar had spilled the punch. She smiled and extended her gloved hand, then drew it back, removed the glove, then extended it again. It was gesture of courtesy but an exaggerated one, designed, I realised later, to make me feel even more inferior. Edgar did not seem to notice, but Frank and I decided when we were walking home later on that she was to be regarded with caution. All night she seemed to be appraising me, her eyes playful and mocking, and not knowing if she was ever serious or not made me feel uncomfortable.

We met up regularly for months afterwards, at the Eureka and other places all around the city. Then Frank went back to base and I stayed in the flat we had secured, because accommodation at that time was so hard to come by we decided we couldn't afford to let it go. I told the landlady that he would be back at any time, and I know she wasn't approving, but she put up with it so long as I paid her rent. Something about her was hostile to young women living on their own, which was strange considering she was on her own too. I suppose she had earned it, with her husband long dead and her children grown up and gone away. Anyway, I found work in a department store, using my maiden name and not wearing my wedding ring to avoid being sacked. So long as Frank was away it was all quite possible. And of course when he was sent to Korea, and then killed, there was no longer any need for pretence. Extraordinary how much more a widow was respected than a married woman. And a widow was not respected all that much, I can assure you.

Over the next couple of years I lost touch with Edgar, since we were no longer two couples. Those days of the four of us spending nights out dancing were over by then. And all that time I'd had no idea that there was a brother until Edgar contacted me again. He came up to me at the notions counter in David Jones. I was surprised to see how he had aged in just a few years. He looked thinner, and his hair was already greying. He told me he had married Catherine and that Cliff had appeared at the wedding, unexpected. 'From the day we were married,' he told me, 'my life changed.' He was both happier and far more miserable than he imagined possible.

Catherine took a great and abiding joy out of living. She always wanted to have fun, and as Edgar's life had been so sober and steady this took him by surprise. Infatuation made him indulge his wife, or refashion his idea of what a wife should be. She loathed living in Ashfield, the house being far too gloomy and old for her liking. She wanted to move somewhere fancy, Rose Bay or Manly, somewhere on the beach, and he promised to do everything he could to move, although he had to stay where the bank wanted him. He would often come home from work to find she'd done nothing but browse the shops in town for the entire day. Or she would skip off on a whim, sometimes taking the train up to the Blue Mountains. She'd return after dark, breathless, her face burnished by the crisp air, laughing at his concern and teasing him for sitting in the cold kitchen waiting for dinner. She would heat up a tin of soup and make toast and they pretended they were camping somewhere, making do.

He told me they had been married for about a year when one night Catherine did not come home at all. He sat up all night with the light on in the front window. He left for work as usual the next morning, stopping by the police station to report her missing. When he returned home that afternoon she was waiting for him, in a fury. How dare he try to alarm people! How humiliating it was for her to be met at Strathfield train station by a police officer and escorted home as if she were a common criminal. They had an argument, shouting in the kitchen, which culminated in her slapping him on the cheek and locking herself in their bedroom. He sat up in a chair in the sitting room all night.

After that she did exactly as she pleased. She played housewife for days at a time, presenting Edgar with platters of butterfly cakes and coconut macaroons, sweet things he did not care for, or cooking up great stockpots full of soups or enough stew to feed a family of ten, which would have to be thrown out into the garden at the back. Meanwhile her jaunts continued. Up the coast to Woy Woy, or Cardiff. Down to Kiama to see the blowhole. She would return, radiant, her eyes bright with excitement and Edgar learned not to question, never to argue, to wait patiently until she came home. He loved her so much he would allow her anything.

It did not occur to him that she was even seeing Cliff, let along spending time away with him. Cliff hinted that he had made quite a handsome amount of money, and no one was ever sure where or how, but by the time of his brother's marriage he had returned from another long trip away. And he always had cash to spare. One Sunday morning he appeared in their street driving a new Chevrolet Stylemaster, sky blue. People came out of their houses to have a look. He took Catherine off for a spin, as he called it, and Edgar waited all through lunchtime, spending the afternoon clipping the hedge and mowing the lawn at the back, for something to do. He was doing the edges with hand shears, on his knees in the afternoon shade, when he heard the sound of the Chevrolet out in the street. He stood up and went to the gate to see Cliff escorting his wife out of the car with exaggerated courtesy. They were both laughing. When his brother spotted him, in old khaki shorts and stained Chesty Bonds, he lifted his hat to him.

'Come on in,' Catherine said gaily. 'I'll make us all cheese on toast.'

Cliff had brought two bottles of dark ale, which he held up in each hand with a shrug and a smile as if to say to Edgar, Hell, it wasn't my fault, but your wife's such a devil for fun, before following her down the hall and into the kitchen. Her feet clattered loudly on the polished floorboards. Even going for a Sunday drive she wore her best heels.

Edgar stood at the door. 'There's no bread,' he said.

Catherine had forgotten to order it. Or been out when the baker came.

'Never mind, Edgar. We'll have a drink anyway!' She hummed as she sniffed at a block of cheese she took out of the refrigerator. Cliff poured three ales and sat down at the kitchen table.

Holding one up he said, 'Good health!' and winked at his brother like this was the greatest lark ever. Edgar was still standing at the doorway, shears in hand.

'Well, I'll go and get changed,' he said.

*

YOUR FATHER WAS BLIND STUPID, for an intelligent man. He was thrilled beyond words when Catherine announced she was expecting, and devoted himself to her as much as he possibly could, despite his work obligations. He was promised a promotion to manager of a much larger branch. She was ill during the pregnancy, and for a long time was virtually an invalid, suffering from the terrible nausea you hear about that afflicts some women all the way through. For the first few months she lost weight, rather than gained it, and remained confined to her bed for most of the time. Edgar engaged a girl to come and care for her for part of the day, and every evening when he returned from work he would warm up the meal she had prepared and serve Catherine something, beef broth or scrambled eggs, light food that she could manage to keep down. She was worse during the day, and in the mornings. I would have come and helped out too, but by that stage she would have none of it. Possibly she could bear to meet me when we were all together, but in her own house, when she was invalided, it was unthinkable. Frank had been more suspicious of her than I, and she disliked him even more I think.

It seemed that as soon as they were married, Catherine had changed. Or she was the same, but an exaggerated version of herself: she was highly strung, people would say, easily excitable and quick to fall into one of her black moods. Now I suppose she would have been called a depressive. Not that this entirely accounted for her behaviour, in my view.

I did drop in occasionally, for old times' sake and because I genuinely cared for Edgar, we both did, Frank and I. I'd visit on my way home after work, in the late afternoon, when I knew that Edgar would be arriving home too, and stay for a cup of coffee or sometimes not even that. Once when I arrived I saw the Chevrolet Stylemaster parked ahead of me in the street. It was impossible to avoid the meaning of that, but I walked up to the house anyway, to see the girl, Milly, just leaving for the day. She came towards me and we spoke for a few minutes at the gate before I entered: she had left the front door open for me. I walked in to see Cliff emerging from the bedroom and featuring what can only be described as a smirk. I could have slapped his self-satisfied face. As always, I said little to him and went in to Catherine who was sitting on the edge of the bed, and dressed as if she planned on going out, aside from her slippers. As soon as she saw me she sighed and took her dressing gown off the back of the door and started unbuttoning her dress. She looked remarkably well that day, with colour in her cheeks.

'Put the kettle on would you, Nell,' she said, turning her back on me to continue undressing. 'I could drink some weak tea.' From outside I heard the throaty purr of the Chevrolet as it pulled out.

By the time Edgar arrived home shortly afterwards she was back in bed, sulking and complaining about her health. 'Another few months, my love,' he said, sitting beside the bed and holding her hand. 'I'm sure you can manage.' She pressed her lips and said nothing. I took in her tea and left. I had seen enough.

There were a few more episodes like this: I will not bother with the shabby details. Needless to say I saw even less of that family, if that's what it was, and kept to myself. Frank was still away and I could have spent a lot more time helping them, or Catherine, but my help was not what she wanted. Or she wanted me for certain things only. One evening I had a parcel to deliver, some curtains that she'd asked me to have made up at work weeks before, so I was obliged to take them around.

Sometimes you see the entire story in mere seconds, and then the story stays with you, swelling to fill your mind until your head might burst. Even if it is one of the oldest stories in the book.

It was just after dark and when I approached I saw the three of them in the front sitting room, a corner lamp all that lit it up. Edgar's figure, his back to me, was standing over Catherine, then he moved out of the door to reveal her and Cliff seated on either end of the couch. As soon as he left, Cliff slid across to embrace her. He was quicker than a lizard. As he placed his hand on her stomach she looked away from him and directly into my face. Her eyes glittered, catching the light from that one lamp. She laid her hand over his and stared at me through the window. I dropped my parcel on the porch, turned around and walked away as quickly as I could.

*

I FELT SORRY FOR EDGAR, but angry with him too. He was a decent man, but he was smart and I couldn't understand how he didn't see what was so clearly evident. She must have been only a few weeks off giving birth when I saw him again. I was home one Sunday afternoon, when he knocked. I was very surprised to see him, I must admit, since I wasn't even aware that he knew where I lived. My first thought was that the landlady would object, then I realised she would be out visiting her sister. Even so I was wary since she was a difficult, censorious woman, always hinting that she knew my husband was away.

I was just completing a shawl I had been knitting for the past few weeks. It was in beautiful cream baby merino that the supervisor of haberdashery had let me have for half price. Despite everything I decided I would finish it and hand it over after the birth.

Edgar was agitated about Catherine. He kept telling me how worried he was about her, how sick she had been. He felt she would not cope with the birth, and wanted to know if I could be around to help her. I think even then he was unaware of how much his wife disliked me, and had not seemed to notice that I'd put myself in the background as a consequence. He reminded me that she had no family to turn to, that she was very much alone and had few friends in Sydney. He refused my offer of a cup of tea or coffee, and kept prattling on and on about how delicate she was, how much she had suffered, how she needed support. Finally he mentioned Cliff.

'Clifford's been wonderful,' he said, 'visiting as often as he can and taking Catherine out for drives when she feels well enough.' He went on until I could not stand it a second longer.

'Edgar, are you that blind?' I said. 'This is insane.'

'What do you mean?' He seemed genuinely puzzled.

'I mean, can't you see what is right under your nose? Your wife is not that sick. She is simply having a difficult pregnancy, it happens all the time.'

He blinked repeatedly.

'And what do you think she and Cliff are up to, spending all that time together?'

At that he became enraged. He stood up, his brow dark. His mouth pressed shut then opened once or twice like a faulty valve, until it finally opened properly and he shouted at me.

'How dare you insinuate anything about Catherine!'

I stood up too. 'I don't dare anything. I just know what I see.'

He grabbed his hat and went to the door. 'What would you know! You're just jealous.'

'Jealous! Of your selfish, spoiled wife?'

'Yes, jealous. Bitter. Married five years and no baby.'

For a moment I was unable to speak with shock and he was already out the door before I found my voice again.

'I could say the same about you.'

He whipped around. 'What do you mean?'

'You don't have a baby either. What makes you think it's yours?'

I slammed the door behind him and stood behind it. Fury had made me breathless. I almost expected him to pound on the door and demand that I explain myself, but all I heard were his long strides taking him down the driveway and out to the street.

I made myself a gin and tonic but even after I drank it I felt bad. I felt like tossing the shawl into the rubbish bin but sat down and put the radio on and finished the lace stitch edging, forcing my fingers to stop trembling. When it was done later that night I packed it away. After I began looking after you I realised it was my gift to you, not her, and so I wrapped you in it right from the start.

The next afternoon when I returned from work my landlady was waiting to see me. She said nothing but handed me an envelope: a notice to quit.

*

I ALWAYS IMAGINED that deep inside Edgar knew, but that so long as no one articulated it he could pretend it wasn't true.

A couple of months later I found him at Ashfield, alone and in the dark. It was as if he was squatting in that house. Catherine always resented being there and was never a homemaker, but when she left all the light and life seemed to vanish from it. I think the electricity was not working, or had been disconnected. He'd been washing in a cold tub and eating his meals in the café near the bank. He stood behind the screen door, looking sadder than anyone I had ever seen.

'I'm sorry,' I told him. 'I had no right.'

He shrugged and invited me in. We sat in the kitchen drinking Scotch and water out of old Mrs Shaw's best Stuart crystal tumblers, dusty though they were.

'He visited in the hospital a couple of days afterwards,' Edgar said. 'When he picked the baby up I saw him and Catherine look at each other. Then I knew it was true.'

He didn't say these words to reassure me. They still sounded as toxic as when I had told him. I knew that my words had cracked open the hard shell of Edgar's understanding, and had I never confronted him like that, then he may never have seen that look over the hospital bed.

'I left straight after that,' he added. 'I couldn't bear it.'

Then he put his head down and cried and cried, great heaving sobs, almost tearless, but as though his chest was going to break apart.

'Edgar,' I finally said, 'you have to go and claim that child.'

You would have been about six weeks old by then. He'd left that very night, walked out of the hospital ward and disappeared for two weeks until coming back to the house that was so cold and lonely. He'd had no contact at all but presumed Catherine and Cliff were at his flat, with you. I was beginning to feel a mild alarm. Catherine was no mother, and Edgar, I knew, would be the best father you could ever have. 'She needs you,' I added, 'that baby. Cliff might have fathered her but she's yours. Your daughter.'

He pressed his hands to his eyes as if he feared they might escape from their sockets, then took his hands away and looked at me. 'I'll need you to come with me,' he said.

I agreed.

'And I'll need your help afterwards.'

I agreed to that too. I felt it was the least I owed him. I had been staying with a friend, in her spare room. It was a cheerless situation, for she was not well off and was expecting her third child. Her husband, a semi invalid, was already hinting about when I might find a place of my own.

We arranged to meet at Cliff's Petersham flat the following week. He walked me up the hall to the front door. The house was completely dark by then. He promised he would have the electricity and gas reconnected, and in return I offered to go shopping for bottles and formula, and all the other basics.

'He brought her in three dozen red roses, you know. To the hospital. *Three* dozen.' He laughed, a humourless laugh. 'The nurses had trouble finding enough vases.'

*

IT WAS AS IF CATHERINE was ready and waiting for us. The place seemed almost empty, spare, not that it had ever been anything more than a bachelor's flat. Cliff was nowhere to be seen. She opened the door when Edgar knocked, turned around and walked back inside without saying a word. Your father went straight over to where you were asleep in the corner of the sitting room, in the white pram which he had bought months before. He had bought most of the baby things, despite the fact it was she who loved to shop.

I was waiting at the door but she appeared again, coming close where she practically hissed at me, glaring up, for even in her heels she could never surmount her dainty height.

'If it wasn't for your interference,' she said, 'everything would have been all right.' She held my eyes as she pulled on her gloves, then turned away to go, adjusting the tilt of her hat in the hall mirror. Edgar was gazing at you. It was the first time he'd seen you since the hospital. Out of the corner of my eye I noticed him carefully reach in and pick you up. I would not turn and watch him, and be a witness to the tears creeping down his face.

In front of the mirror she turned this way and that, checking out her appearance, smoothing down the fabric of her frock over her stomach. She looked very self-satisfied, despite her anger. Watching her fix her makeup, I gained the distinct impression that all her sickness throughout the pregnancy had been somehow concocted, as if she had been trying her hardest to expel all trace of a baby from her body. When she was done smacking her lips together she snapped her handbag shut and brushed past me without another word, let alone a glance behind her.

Strangely, Cliff was not waiting for her in the car. I could hear her heels clicking angrily all the way up the footpath.

32

AT HER DESK DOVE LET OUT A GREAT long sigh. Then she closed the laptop and sat back in her chair. Her back ached. It was nearly midday and she would get up and have an early lunch. She was tired. She kept waking suddenly in the early hours to realise that the abortion she had seemed to experience along with her character was just an invention. Or that Ellis had never opened that box to discover a photo of her mother taken when she was married and seen that the resemblance between them was nothing short of shocking. Or that the baby, Charlie, never existed.

In the kitchen she made herself a strong coffee. But as she pressed the plunger it gurgled then spewed up, spraying her T-shirt with hot mud.

'Fuck. Fucking fucking fuck!'

Viv sat in the corner and curled his tail around his body, regarding her with slit eyes.

'Fuck it,' she said again but much quieter.

She tossed the plunger into the sink, wiped the bench and washed her hands, then went to her bedroom to change. She needed to get out. She would go into town, David Jones or somewhere, and buy a proper coffee maker, a good quality espresso machine. It was ridiculous that she, a writer, should be depriving herself of something as basic as decent coffee. And it was not like she could not afford it. Yet as soon as she thought that she felt guilty, and then felt angry with herself for such stupid pettiness. Her mother would not have begrudged her the best espresso machine one could buy. But every time she considered something special she couldn't shake off the idea that this was an extravagance she did not deserve, and mere exploitation of the profits of her mother's death.

She knew what the problem was, she thought on the bus into town. She should never have left her job, painful though it had become. And she had forgotten to be careful what she wished for. She had taken advantage of not needing to work for the first time in her life. Lately, she had written every day and decided that only after finishing this novel would she think about getting another job. There would be no pressure. She wouldn't have to worry about a thing, all the bills would be paid, she could even take time off from this job of being a writer – the one that didn't pay – go away on holidays for a week or two, and work from home in a disciplined manner. And when the story was finished she would then acquire an agent and only after that look around for a new position, something part time in design again that would perhaps allow her to work on a new project. She was not foolish enough to imagine she would find a new job as a writer.

But she had been foolish enough to think she exercised some control over the story. Now that it had made her back ache and confounded her to the point she wanted to yell at people who simply did not exist, she knew she understood very little about what she was doing. She wished she had never imagined this story, that she could wind the clock back to before that first dream when she saw Ellis travelling on the bus – just like she was now, how infuriating was that? – to visit her father, and understood this was one small scene out of a much larger story.

In the past few months she had twice decided it would never work, and ignored the story. To distract herself, she had decided to pursue activities that she had never done before, and so enrolled in a meditation course at a local alternative therapy centre, and taken up motorcycle riding. This latter involved a proper course of instruction and was a great deal harder than she envisaged. She had bought a second-hand motor scooter and found that riding out along the quiet back streets of some suburbs, where she felt safer, the marvellous, easy freedom did not stop her mind roaming back into the story. She went to weekly meditation classes for three months and practised at home every afternoon, but while she knew meditation was meant to empty her mind, she could not control the images that crowded in. Invariably she found that after going for a ride, say out to Breakfast Point where the streets were quiet and clean and safe to the point of being eerie, she would return home only to go straight to the story, a scene fresh in her head.

In meditation classes, more than once the instructor had leaned close to her, when she was seated cross-legged, her eyes closed, and whispered, 'Dove, stay in the moment please. Concentrate on the flame only.' How did she know, Dove wondered, that she was not visualising the candle flame that had been placed before them in the intimate and darkened room with the seagrass matting, but that she was looking directly at a dark green tin box? Or a girl sitting on her bed hugging her knees? Her head had remained full of questions and gaps in the narrative. Where was Ellis now? The question of what had happened to Charlie. When Edgar had died. And the mystery that loomed like swollen thunderclouds in almost every scene in her head: why Ellis's mother had left.

She did not assume for a minute that now she had found the answers to these questions, the story would leave her alone.

By the time she reached the city she had made a decision. She would look for a new position, even if it was part time. She had to – to preserve her sanity. Only the other day Martin had mentioned that someone he knew working on one of the magazines was looking for new designers. At David Jones she bought a Saeco espresso machine, ridiculously expensive for one person's use, big and complex enough to serve a café, and ordered it to be delivered. Afterwards she went down to the food hall and bought some fennel, rocket and organic chicken sausages and a tub of beetroot and Persian feta salad for dinner. She walked across to George Street and down to Dymocks, deciding to spend only ten minutes there before going home.

It was like a conspiracy. Facing her just inside the doorway was a stand of Penguin classic reprints, and in the middle of the top shelf was a copy of *Wuthering Heights*.

33

⁋ IT WAS THE FINAL WEEK OF ELLIS'S JOB.
Of her career. A massive restructuring meant there would
no longer be an executive editor or managing editor of *Pages*
magazine. Those roles were taken by the publishing director of
the magazine section of the company, now just part of a diverse
media empire owned by shareholders. The vice-president by
this time had died, a heart attack, the same as his father, though
no one now kept shrines to them in the former executive
level offices. The magazine production staff had shrunk over
the years, and the premises had changed again. Ellis's office
had gone from being open plan, to a proper office, back to
open plan: it was half glassed in, now a big shared space with
the art director and fashion editor at their own uncluttered
glass desks nearby. All of them were part time by this stage.

She had been working three days a week for the last few years.

Ellis was content to be leaving. She had been here for so many decades the joke was she was part of the furniture. Beneath the jokes she detected a fluttering of criticism from the younger staff that she had not left say ten years ago when that would have been more seemly, for a woman of her position. It was not as if she needed the money. And what dinosaurs didn't change jobs every three years or so?

It was true she had had to cope with enormous changes. There were no more senior writers, and all the contributors were now freelance, every one of them. The women's pages that had occupied her at the very start of her job had long gone, for they were anachronistic, but Ellis still missed the interaction with readers those pages had offered. Not that she wanted those pages back, but she could not help feeling a stir of nostalgia for the section that had brought her into the industry. It was not fanciful to say that this job had saved her sanity. Right from the start she had found even the most mundane tasks useful. She had proofread like no one else, the most scrupulous proofreader the magazine had ever employed. She read through every single dull, self-important letter from readers, even the ones that offered recipes for the most basic dishes, white sauce or meatballs. There was no task back then that she thought too unworthy, she tackled everything with care. Valerie had, she now thought, resented her willingness to take on anything, as if she were sucking up to the management.

In her last week she was sifting through her personal papers, though in the office she had shared for the last few years, there'd not been much room for paper. Her laptop sat beside the company's desktop computer on her glass-topped desk. A poster of the fiftieth anniversary issue cover of *Pages*, featuring Mike Walsh and Kylie Minogue, then the outgoing and rising stars of popular television, in a celebratory embrace, decorated the far wall of the offices.

Pages magazine was being redesigned. The executive editor had already decided from the three different concepts the new designer had sent through: there was to be a lot more white space, clearer delineation between headlines, pull quotes and body copy. Typography was going to be treated a great deal more seriously, as was photography, though there was to be a lot less of that. In the meetings to discuss the revamping Ellis had thought the emphasis was too much on style over content, but the executive editor insisted they were on the right track. People wanted quality not quantity, he said. Readers were sick of sound bites and web pages. They were becoming bored with swiping pages with their fingers. And they no longer wanted throwaway papers. They would pay for a quality production, that's what the research said. There were no new contributors or content editors. The journalists, the writers, all freelance, were always referred to as content providers. She could not remember when that had happened, exactly, or how, just that it was irreversible.

And she could not recall the last time she had spoken with a feature writer. Once the magazine had boasted half-a-dozen of them, all eminent, some award-winning writers in their different fields: arts, sport, travel writing. Now copy arrived via the mothership of the company, some of it seeming not to have a by-line until she made enquiries. It was her job simply to arrange it, and oversee production. Indeed she could not recall the last time she had had the luxury of commissioning a piece. And soon the pages would be determined entirely by design. The new designer would be coming in later that morning, to discuss handover issues. There was also the suggestion of a name change, but so far no one had provided a better alternative.

She placed a pile of old proofs into the recycling box by the door. These she had kept for nostalgic reasons as they were the last pages to be set in hard copy, before they shifted to computerised layout. They had used a clear glue – what was its name? – and their offices were always littered with slivers of paper. Another set of proof pages was bristling with pink Post-it notes, with corrections and comments written in purple ink, in her own hand. What on earth had they done before Post-it notes were invented? She could not remember that either.

There was no door to Ellis's office. Sitting in her chair at her desk, she could see straight towards the lift where on either side were posters of other memorable *Pages* covers: a royal visit, Charles and Diana with a baby; a former prime minister with his younger second wife. Both covers emphasised the colour gold – was that deliberate? she couldn't remember – and from this distance the blocky playful capitals of the magazine title looked absurdly old-fashioned. A few years previously, they changed it to Didot, with its clean and clever contrast of fine and strong lines. Along with the magazine's simple crisp title, Didot offered just a suggestion of classical design without sacrificing its contemporary edge. The design team then had been very clever, she thought. If *Pages* had still been the *Women's Pages*, it simply would not have worked. That would have demanded a more flowing, or more relaxed type. In which case they may as well have stuck with Cooper Black, which is what it was when Ellis began. Design changed too rapidly now. A look or a style became tired within five years.

She had once been fascinated by typography. There was that time when she'd applied for a job at a printer's workshop, naively expecting to be able to design type. Instead she had used type in ways she had never imagined, but she had still never designed a typeface as she'd once hoped to do. Since the mid-1980s they had called them fonts, not typefaces, and of all of them on the company's Apple Macs, she still preferred the default one, New York. Now for some reason New York had been banished from the fonts menu. Venice, with a look that to her suggested gondolas; Los Angeles, almost handwritten; Chicago, which she loathed with an irrational passion – all the fonts named after cities that Steve Jobs had loved – they were now inexplicably gone. Once she had even considered resurrecting Doves from a hundred years back, the typeface that she and Tom had talked about, the first day they met. All that research she had done on the topic of typefaces, late at night, using books she borrowed from the local library. The creator of Doves had kept it in his heart, even though he'd drowned it.

Ellis had a strange compulsion to tear down everything she could from all her years at *Pages* and keep them for herself. An irrational desire. It was merely a popular magazine, a glossy with attitude, or an evening frock in sensible shoes as the former fashion editor had put it. It had kept her busy all these years, used her skills, paid the rent, and had not been without its battles. Yet now the end was here she felt a fierce affection, a possessiveness, for what she had achieved. She looked around the office. If all the issues she had ever worked on were here before her she would have tried to take them in her arms and run away with them.

Ellis was not an emotional woman. Ever since she was quite young she had firmly kept the lid upon her sensibilities and stayed calm when others had not. She had fought with no one at work, retreated from petty office dramas, engaged in little that would suck her energy and leave her spent. She had preserved herself, she realised. And that was what people would call her now, she thought, behind her back. Well preserved, like a jar of cumquats. Now she felt an unaccustomed desire to wilt. She sat at her desk, slumped back into her chair and pulled out the last drawer to be cleared.

It was uncharacteristically messy with receipts, manuscript articles, news clippings, letters, bills and cards. It was the drawer she reserved for things she thought she ought to keep, or might want to look at later, though either rarely proved to be the case. The envelope was addressed to her at work, and could have been opened then regummed over the years. She recognised the handwriting.

Dear Ellis,

You have probably thought there was no more to the story I told you some years ago, when we last spoke. Before you become alarmed, let me assure you that as far as your life is concerned, I have told you all that you needed (and deserved) to know. All I told you was the truth.

But I was not truthful when I told you that I was seventeen when I had my abortion. I was much older than that. And it was after Frank was killed.

I was a widow, you understand, and there was no possibility of keeping it.

I lodged with you and Edgar until you were nearly three. If you have any early memories of a woman in that house (as I suspect you have) then it was not your mother as you always hoped, but me. I kept to myself as far as I could, sleeping next to your room. The news about Frank was as devastating as you could imagine. For so much of our married life we had been apart and I grieved for all the wasted time as much as I grieved for him.

Simply, your father and I were both lonely. But there was no question of us marrying. Your father would be forever infatuated with your mother. A marriage based on mutual bitter disappointment was not what either of us desired. And a marriage made from compromise . . . Well, that is something you understand can crush you flat. I would remain a widow. There would be no baby. My experience was a lot more messy and dangerous than yours, but I survived.

Afterwards I could not bear to be in the house when he was. You might remember that as soon as he came home from work I would put on my hat and coat and leave. He found the flat for me down the road, and paid the rent for the first few years, until I insisted otherwise. But I agreed to keep looking after you because I owed him. And I owed you, for if I had not intervened, then maybe, just maybe, your mother would not have gone away. Please forgive me, Ellis.

You will understand how some words are impossible to say, which is why I have written this in a letter to be sent to you after my death. You will, I hope, understand that I did not wish to see you again, after telling you all that I have. I think you know that I have always had your welfare in mind, and hope you recall fondly the years we spent together when you were young and your father at work. I certainly have. Indeed those memories are the only thing that have sustained me, all these years.
Kindest regards,
Nell Wood

34

⸂ A RITUALISTIC CLEARING OF HER DESK the night before was followed by a dinner. She treated herself to a whole night out. She had a meeting the next morning at the magazine, a formality but still important, even though she'd all but got the contract. She went to Passageway, again crowded with after-work drinkers, but she didn't mind not being able to talk to Martin. He waved at her from the other side of the bar, she called out, 'I think I've finished that story!' and he smiled and gave her the thumbs-up.

There were a few people there she'd been chatting to in the past few months. They shared a bottle of wine and talked about the government and the strangely apocalyptic weather and agreed they were both related, then she went and ate Thai.

She returned home slightly drunk to find the cat sitting on her desk, refusing to jump down, and she didn't mind this either. The new copy of *Wuthering Heights* was still out. She picked it up. An astonishing and unexpected thought gripped her: now that she was done with it, and here was a new clean copy, she might even read it again. It would be different to reading her mother's copy of the novel, the one she'd taken into her in hospital then brought home again. She'd only just unpacked the box of possessions from that time, now more than a year ago. What she had brought back from those months in hospital was so little, almost nothing to represent a woman's life even in her dying weeks. Jane's reading glasses, purse, hand cream, her Classic Coral lipstick – and the annotated copy of the novel that had started it all.

It was impossible to be resentful. Emily Brontë had written this novel especially for her. For her benefit she had sat alone in her narrow bed in the parsonage, her lap desk on her knees, death all around her with that graveyard right next door, the cold wind from the moors behind rattling the windows. She should be grateful. For her Emily had made Catherine say the words, *It would degrade me to marry Heathcliff . . . I am Heathcliff.* She was grateful. Of course Emily had written it for her alone.

But for whom had Dove written her story? Apart from herself.

35

⸿ SHE FOLDED THE LETTER AND REPLACED it in its envelope. *Kindest regards.* Nell Wood had bathed her scraped knees with Dettol and warm water, and wiped her tears and blown her nose. For months she had sat patient and rigid on a blue metal chair in the cold School of Arts dance room while Ellis stumbled about learning ballet. She had guided her hand drawing her loops and hooks practising running writing after school. She had confided her dearest domestic secrets to Ellis: a good pinch of salt would bring out the flavour in hot chocolate; knitting into the back of the first row of stitches made a much neater band; eucalyptus oil was the best thing for removing sticky labels from jars.

How had this letter been misplaced all these years? Nell Wood had died fifteen years ago. She had been to the funeral, a quiet service in the crematorium chapel, with a handful of the Grange staff, herself the only mourner from outside. She thought and thought about it, but quite honestly Ellis now had no idea whether she had read it and immediately suppressed it, or if it had arrived one day among a whole lot of other mail for the magazine and become mislaid and forgotten in the drawer.

She tossed it into the box of things she was taking home, then took it out again, considering whether after all this time she really needed it, or even cared. She was still holding it when the woman walked out of the lift, directly ahead of her. She recognised herself in her at once: the same penetrating blue eyes, the same dark hair, the way she jerked her bag over her left shoulder as she strode across the room. The baby, the girl, the woman she had always thought of as Columbine walked straight up to Ellis and looked her in the face before she spoke, shaking her head in wonder and disbelief.

'I've imagined you for so long,' Dove said. 'I can hardly believe that here you are.'

AUTHOR'S NOTE

The Women's Pages began life in the short story, 'The Sleepers in that Quiet Earth', first published in *Best Australian Stories 2011*, edited by Cate Kennedy (Black Inc, 2011), and reprinted in my collection *Letter to George Clooney* (Picador, 2013); my thanks to the editors of these books for their advice.

I am very grateful to my publisher, Alex Craig, who embraced this novel from the start and reassured my doubts all the way through. I have been fortunate to have wise and insightful editorial input from Ali Lavau and Julia Stiles. Thanks also to Emma Rafferty, editorial manager and excellent traffic controller; and to Therese Scott and Mandy Keevil from Ashfield Library for help with local history.

Doves Type did exist and has now been resurrected. See Simon Garfield's *Just My Type* (Profile Books, 2010). Special thanks to Gregory Ferris for finding Doves Type for my computer; the chapter openings of this novel are in Doves.

A special thank you to Antony for the love and the endless encouragement (and all the dinners). And finally thanks to my daughter Ellen for the beautiful purple notebook and the perfect green chair: I used them both to write this book.

Author photograph: Gregory Ferris